Do Clones Have Souls

Herbert Wright

Copyright © 2008 Herbert Wright

ISBN 978-1-60145-532-1

All rights reserved. No part of this publication may be reproduced, stored in a retrieval system, or transmitted in any form or by any means, electronic, mechanical, recording or otherwise, without the prior written permission of the author.

Printed in the United States of America.

The characters and events in this book are fictitious. Any similarity to real persons, living or dead, is coincidental and not intended by the author.

Booklocker.com, Inc.
2008

Dedication

To Carroll and Lucky Wright, I was truly blessed to have you both. I would have to write another book just to thank you for all you have done for me. To the Cole family, Diane and Lisa, Kenneth and Terrell Sis and Babe thank you for the many ways you made my life better.

To Roger, Spell, Charles, Vincent, Leo and Stan, my CCNY family, and the many political junkies and social critics who helped to refine my ideas in verbal jousts over many years.

To my family Gerry, Kirby and Lena who greet me like a returning war hero when I come home from work. You are all better than I deserve or ever expected.

Chapter One

I awaken startled, my eyes darting in the dark. I hear a sound, faint and repetitive, and quickly lift my head. It's clearer now--footsteps. I move quietly and listen intently as I slide my legs from under the blanket. I maneuver carefully, hoping to avoid the betrayal of a squeaky mattress.

Damn, how did they find me? No time to think. I ease off the bed and slip into my clothes. I move to the window, using my finger to lift the curtain, and peek out at the street. I clear my eyes. Night is surrendering to day.

BOOM! The shotgun blast merges with the sound of shattering glass as I leap through the window.

The descent from the third story to the top of the blue convertible seems endless; I can't breathe, and butterflies swarm in my belly. I turn sideways and brace myself. I feel the impact and then bounce again on the top of the car. Everything inside me feels instantly sore and permanently changed, but to stay is to die. I roll off the canvas roof of the car as the second blast sears through the top of the La Baron and the hood. Holding my arm, I limp into an alley across the street. I run and walk until I find a place to rest. I will live another day.

I awaken in a subway tunnel; pain and danger prevent me from sleeping soundly. I have lived in the streets now for almost two years. It has been so long since I had elegant meals and restful sleep that I cannot imagine having them again. I used to remember those things fondly and with yearning. Now I am like a man who accepts that he is blind and wishes he had no memory of sight.

I struggle to get up, stepping deliberately. I move around and between others who are sleeping; I evade those who lurk in the dark to do harm. Here children compete with rats for food; they steal quickly--using surprise--darting in and out of openings of this huge cave too many call home.

I head up the stairs toward light, to what used to be a subway entrance, now boarded up. I bend, stick one leg through an opening in the boards and contort my body so that I can slip through to the other side.

I straighten up slowly, stiffly, out of danger now, but my pain harshly reasserts itself. My right leg and shoulder are throbbing and my ribcage feels like it will explode when I breathe. I am forced to take shallow, deliberate breaths. I pass a store window where I check myself out; I see dried blood under my nose, on my neck, and entangling hair at the top of my chest. I raise my shirt and see the bluish-purple bruise on my ribs. I touch it carefully; it is swollen and tender but it does not seem broken. Although painful, I know the injuries will heal.

There is another ache that rises to the surface; it is the pain of hunger. I reflexively put my hand in my pocket and then remember that I keep my money in my sock so no one will steal it when I sleep. I wear tight shoes, as well, since shoes are in high demand.

People like me used to be called hobos or bums. Then in the 1970s and 80s there was a surge of poor and mentally ill people without shelter who were called homeless. Now that so many formerly middle-class people share this existence, we are called Transitionals. I don't think it matters much what we are called.

I have $4,000 left, the only remnants of better days. I go to a local Mega-bath where up to fifty can wash, shave and change. These places are always crowded and people take too long, but it beats restrooms in diners and bus stations. I like the fact that you can lock them from the inside and you don't have to watch your clothes. They have guards here too.

Mega-baths sprang up as part of the large national protest by Transitionals. As a result, Congress enacted the Save Our American People Act. One of the rights it established was the right to be clean. We heard dozens of speeches about the dignity of all citizens, talk about how cleanliness would reduce disease and how applicants would look better for job interviews. With great fanfare, the contract to build Mega–baths was awarded to one of our nation's four remaining corporations in 2023. It is hard to believe that was only two years ago.

I emerge feeling clean and refreshed. As I walk I'm thinking that when I sit down to eat I'm going to ask for ice. I'm going to use it for my ribs and to put on my head to ease the swelling and to let water trickle down my neck, to cool me in this heat.

It is the end of August. Soon it will be Golden Quarter, the time from September to December that retailers associate with good holiday business. To Transitionals it means that the brutal heat of summer has ended and the cold harshness of winter has yet to assert itself. As I begin to think about sizzling bacon and cheesy eggs, my mouth waters and my stomach cramps. I decide to take my mind off food and look up, just in time. At the corner across the street I see a horde of men. The cramp in my stomach is replaced by a nervous tingling. The street is fairly crowded; The horde scans the crowd for potential victims .

Years ago, when I watched nature shows as a child, I always felt sorry for the antelope that got plucked from the pack. Like the antelope herd we moved nervously, with panicked eyes, our circumstances as random and brutal as nature itself.

A few people have already turned around and are walking quickly in the other direction. Others like me keep walking and hoping. Three people begin to run, which starts the charge of the horde. I cannot run; I stand as tall and straight as I can. I am wounded and know that looking weak adds to the danger. In an instant, dreams of ice and eggs could be shattered if these men decide to make me their prey.

I manage to sneak behind a group that is resisting them, passing by, my back sliding across the storefront. I make brief eye contact with a man who starts to point at me but at that moment is punched by one of the resistors. My heart races as I slither around the corner. "AAAAH, AAAH," I repeat softly. Blocks away between buildings, I am bent over trying to breathe, my ribs victims of each full breath. My dream is much smaller now; I just want to breathe without pain.

I finally arrive at one of the Compassionate Light Diners. They have replaced soup kitchens and are a church-business collaboration that efficiently feeds the public. Everyone is fed for a moderate fee (no one should eat for free). Those who cannot pay, work a day of service in factories. This is one of the strategies that "Keeps American employers at home," and reduces outsourcing and the trade imbalance.

Even if you have no home or no job you can still serve America. To some it is their only source of pride. This was also part of the Save Our American People Act. It stated that as part of living with dignity, any paying citizen has the right to two healthy meals or snacks per day.

There are three options at the Diner. The smallest and most expensive meal is the one that by law must be provided. It consists of vegetables, grains and broiled fish or meat. The second is a pre-packaged meal like the Army's C-rations and the third is a mix of foods, served hot. It is food that has reached or just passed its expiration date. It is more plentiful, cheaper and the most popular of the three.

Where you sit is very important. If you sit at the wrong table or if the wrong guy sits next to you, he will eat most of your meal. So many people stand near the guards and eat quickly. They are often victims of pickpockets who move through the crowd; the pickpockets are despised and risk death for a few dollars.

These dangers of dining are rarely a problem for me. I am usually left alone unless there is a big mob or attackers are well armed. I am large, strong, trained in defense and visibly athletic. Where there are so many fragile targets and medical attention so scarce, they would rather not take the chance of being hurt and becoming a victim themselves. I get the small meal and get a cup of ice; I pay the $75 and I am grateful that I do not have to work for food today.

The place smells of hot bread and antiseptic. There is also a less dominant odor of disease, of wounds that did not heal right, of bites that were never treated, of old clothes, feces and vomit. Many of the men and women here are very well educated; others just a few years ago had big houses and nice cars. They watch the large televisions, bolted and chained high on the wall, commenting on the news and telling their children to sit up straight.

As news of progress from War 3 of the Crusade for Religious and Universal Democracy is heard, many cheer. The light flashes red from above the ceiling. Our 20 minutes are finished and it is time for the next group to enter.

As we bump and jostle each other on the way out, as always, a few small fights break out. I think some fight because they are shoulder to shoulder with their worst fears.

A couple tries unsuccessfully to avoid the truck taking those in meal debt to the factory. They receive disdainful looks and comments from those on the truck. "Trying to eat for free, you fucking bum?" "It's because of people like you that our jobs keep going to China, you lazy bitch."

As the truck pulls away, I fear for the couple's safety. A little girl breaks from the crowd, running after the truck and screaming, "Mommy, Daddy." She had been hiding, as directed by her parents, while they tried to escape. She trips and falls in the street. Her father tries to jump out of the truck to pull her aboard but is grabbed and pulled back into his seat by a guard, who clubs him.

A group of teenagers who have just left the Diner mock her, shouting derisively, "Mommy, Daddy." She yells back at them and they start to approach her.

One boy moves behind her, grabs her around the waist and picks her up. He leans back against a parked car, laughing and taunting her as she tries to escape. Her legs are up in the air as she kicks at the boys who now attempt to surround her.

I work my way behind them and get close to two of them who turn around. I smile and yell, "Get her, get her." They turn back around. I hit one in the kidneys and as the other turns I push my knuckles into his eyes. I run straight at the guy with the girl. He drops her to defend himself. She runs, I show him my knife, its over.

He and his other friend grab the two on the ground and take off. As I am walking, I see the girl a few blocks away. I tell her I will walk her back to the diner and tell the guards to give her a ride to the factory.

She says, "I'm hurt."

Her leg has a wide cut that is open and bleeding.

After asking permission I pick her up, and she thanks me. "You remind me of my Daddy, when things were good. He's still nice but he's mad a lot now. You, you're like a Knight in shining armor."

"I'm alright, I guess," I say.

While carrying her I was reminded of two children I cared for in Virginia. Although they were young, they had never faced the challenges and struggles this child faced, not in all their lives.

"Do you have any children?" the girl asked.

"No," I replied.

I doubt that I had ever even been a child myself, surrounded by adults all the time, intellectually the equal of many but having none of their privileges. Children got to play; I never did unless it was as part of some experiment. I envied their freedom, their laughter; I had duties and responsibilities. Mostly I wanted the love that was not given to me. The children's orange dog Ember got more affection than I did. The adults looked at me the way a scientist looks at mice.

It is the way I grew to view the world. I have become a keen observer, a detached wanderer, feeling little more than hunger, curiosity, pain or duty. I eventually overcame my resentment of children and this little one reminded me how charming they could be.

I drop her off, make sure she speaks to the right people and turn to leave. She gives a backward glance and starts to speak but then turns and follows the guard into the building.

As I walk along, thoughts of the children in Virginia fade and my mind turns to thoughts of Sara Khan.

I have not had many close relationships in my life and do not know if I have ever experienced love, but whenever I hear people speak of love I think of her. She is like a quiet fire, mesmerizing, bright, a colorful mix of energy, a safe haven in the darkness.

She is also a world-renowned Healer. I need to feel her warm healing fingers on my body, so wracked with pain. She is the reason I came this city. I will have to walk miles but it has been years since I've seen her and the pain of walking is small compared to the hurt of missing her.

Many people have learned alternative medicine since medical care has become out of reach for most. Some began to treat friends and neighbors and then eventually opened businesses to make a living. There were others who were just con artists.

The HMOs and drug companies used their influence with government to put most Healers out of business, claiming that all Healers were frauds. As a consequence, many Healers now practice underground. They treat people discretely out of legal businesses or as they originated, in people's homes. Regressive Nature is the name of the health food store where Sara heals.

Health food stores have grown in demand. The government's aggressive deregulation of the food industry and the breakdown of environmental protections have been responsible for several highly publicized deaths. This led to State-sponsored class action lawsuits and meteoric stock plunges that destroyed the companies that were most obviously at fault.

It also hurt public trust. People then began to flock to health food stores. The rich and affluent were their best customers. So when the new corporate health boutiques sprang up, Regressive Nature was well positioned for success. The owners were good business people with good hearts, so they also managed Karma, affordable health stores for their growing base of less fortunate customers.

Regressive Nature is a big store. It has three doors and occupies half a block. The first door you enter offers books, audiotapes, crystals and jewelry. The second entrance is an eatery with vegan food and drink and the third door is a grocery where you can buy organic foods, vitamins and herbs. In the back of the grocery are steps to the top floor where classes on meditation, Yoga and massage are held at scheduled times, mostly on weekends.

It is here that Sara Khan discreetly treats the sick and injured. Her attire is an eclectic mix of Native American and African traditions. The large room is decorated with pictures of Buddha, Angels, statues and trinkets. There are small shelves of dusty books and pouches filled with mystery. She has the kind of beauty women pray for; she thinks it gets in the way.

Her given name was Carmen Vasquez. Her mother, Lillian, was in charge of the maids at a Cancun hotel where Carmen spent her early years. Lillian was ambitious and hardworking. She worked long hours in a job that was menial and demanding. She loathed her poverty and her status and while young, dreamt of being pursued by some handsome blond co-ed. She wanted to be an American, able to have anything, like the women in the movies.

Instead she was groped or fondled by guests, if noticed at all. The men she met had one thing on their mind and she was the last resort of an empty evening. No dream could let her give herself so cheaply, so she kept her values and her modesty.

She felt like God was mocking her. Each day she was surrounded by rich, handsome men; each week a new group of young Americans checked into the hotel. "Water, water everywhere but not a drop to drink."

She had a recurring nightmare. In it she reaches for the handsome prince, appearing regal in crown and robe; he contorts into a red-eyed, vomit-breathing monster with eight arms. The scene changes, and she is in the home of her dreams. Her dream man comes out of the shower, body glistening, and says, "Honey I need . . ."

"Yes," she whispers, ". . . more towels."

So she read, improved her English and worked harder than everyone else. It seemed clear to her that if she was going to live as an American, it would be easier to educate herself and apply for citizenship than it would to wait to find the prince in this frog farm. That was her state of mind when she met Carmen's father.

He was a college kid from Princeton planning to attend law school in the fall. He grew up in a Connecticut neighborhood among people of wealth and privilege. He was more interested in sunsets than in parties and despite his charisma and chiseled good looks he spent a lot of time alone.

He was leaving his room that night and saw Lillian and a few of her coworkers departing the hotel. He was interested in eating authentic Mexican food so he asked her in Spanish where he could find good food. The conversation was at first stiff and reserved with probing smiles and gentle eye contact. Soon they began to talk and laugh as if no one was around. One by one her friends departed, offering knowing looks or weak goodbyes.

They decided to have dinner together. Their interest in each other grew exponentially. They lived experiences that would last forever in moments that passed too soon. The night before he left, she made love to him as if her life depended on it. Summoning up all her will and passion, and with the fear of desperation, she clutched him.

At the height of passion her body exploded and her thoughts floated. Her dream was now real, and she felt as if she had burst from a cocoon.

Afterwards, they talked for hours and when there was nothing more to say, she rested her head on his chest and listened to his heart and tried urgently to make their hearts beat together. It is the last thing she remembered as she fell asleep.

But as always the sun came up. Warm goodbyes were made in haste as she prepared for her shift. When he left she did not cry; she held it in and it felt like bleeding.

She knew he would send for her soon. They had loved so hard and said so much. For days and weeks she thought of him, of his sweat, his laugh, his walk. She feared that he had been gone so long that she would forget every detail about him.

She received a few phone calls and letters but it was not the same. She wrote him about her pregnancy and the joy she felt about becoming a family and sharing their lives together in America. But she never saw him again except in her daughter's eyes.

Carmen was not a beautiful baby or a beautiful child. It was as if her genes needed time to homogenize. She was gawky when young, not very coordinated, and tall with a different skin tone than her White and Mexican classmates.

She grew in beauty year by year. Bookish like her mother and father, she wore old black glasses that drooped profoundly on her pointed nose. She had a long neck, tapered waist and delicate hands. Her legs seemed endless, beautifully defined with deep, sharp curves. She tied her hair in a pony-tail that swayed like a pendulum when she walked, lightly brushing her ample behind. Her perfect posture made her hips appear to move independently of her body; everything and everyone else appeared still or out of sync as she glided by with perfect, effortless motion.

Her eyes greeted you and never left you. No matter what was going on in your life, her smile was a moment of pleasure. Men shamelessly stared, wide-eyed and open-mouthed, ruining some vacations before they got started. Women would have hated her except that she was so innocent and loving. Rude drunks, bitter women and delusional would-be suitors were all treated with warmth, respect and charm.

She was, however, defined by her thoughts, which were shaped by the paradox of the staggering poverty of her countrymen and the decadence and hedonism of the hotel's guests. She hated to see people begging for food or enduring backbreaking labor. Many of them lived in houses little more than metal boxes, rusted with exposed wires hanging out; they had little hope here and even fewer dreams. Their reality was as hard as the ground they worked and as unyielding.

The guests spent more on vacations than many families earned in a year. They were tanned, muscular, youthful and often wealthy. Yet unlike her mother, she saw beyond their shiny exteriors. She saw their drunken cravings and heard their slurring confessions. She knew that too many of them were unhappy and she did not envy them at all.

She remembered seeing three girls, obviously drunk but resplendent, wearing the latest designer fashions. They were holding their friend's hair back while she puked colors that did not match. Her face was red, her eyes bulging, her small body convulsing, her friends laughing. No, she did not want to be one of them.

At age sixteen Carmen headed for the Ivy League. Her mother had earned an MBA and was now an assistant hotel manager but she did not have to pay for Carmen's education. Lillian had received a lump sum payment and monthly support from Connecticut since Carmen was born. She insisted that Carmen's tuition for Harvard be paid in full.

Carmen expressed a love of medicine early in her sophomore year. While attending Harvard she met a foreign student from Nigeria named Oye. They became friends while in a study group. He introduced her to a student from China, Ying, who, like the Nigerian, esteemed alternative medicine. She was fascinated by the spiritual genesis of these healing methods and their endurance in traditional cultures. Having accumulated enough credits, she took her junior year off to travel abroad, and her mother agreed to finance the trip.

She traveled to Nigeria with her friend, Oye, and then to Egypt. She was a sponge, soaking in the teachings from sages, grandmothers and local doctors. Later in her life she would be able to viscerally distinguish between the soul types, thought forms, healing and negative energies. It was in Africa that she realized that she had "the calling", "the gift."

After months in Africa, she spent a week with her mother, and then continued her journey of self-discovery. She went to Tibet and Japan. In Tibet, she observed the monks, their centuries old traditions enveloped by strip malls and nightclubs. Each day she talked to the same monk, who was the tour guide for the Monastery. She talked about her sincere desire to learn healing, meditation and philosophy. At first he gave her the same answers he gave all tourists. She returned every day and eventually he relented. She learned to expand her gifts there and experience the deepest of meditations.

Carmen graduated from Harvard Medical School with honors, after which she continued her educational immersion in spiritual healing.

It was seven years after her graduation that I first met Carmen. As an MD and expert in alternative approaches to healing, she had begun to gain recognition for a dual approach to medicine. When she took part in a panel discussion that C-SPAN broadcast on the role of Clones in society, I was in the audience. The panel discussion took place approximately one year after the Life is Unique Resolution of 2015, which allowed the production and utilization of human Clones. The original legislation was very specific and limited, but that changed. Congress and the President were faced with several problems which programmed cloning could address.

We needed troops to fight the wars of Extreme Terror on three fronts. We could use Clones as soldiers. Cloning would also allow us to pay virtually nothing for labor, reversing the outsourcing of American jobs. We could be the world's leading provider of medical transplants customized to order and rise to the forefront as leaders in medical research.

Carmen (who had changed her name to Sara Kahn) had been invited to speak about her view that Clones, from a medical point of view, are human beings and should be treated as such. She was joined on the panel by Dr. Olsen, whose position was that Clones are not human, by Reverend Farend of the religious right and Dr. Algood, an

African- American religious leader. The remaining panelists were from the AFL-CIO, and from WOLF news. The Cambridge Forum presented the discussion; the moderator's name was Noble Concrite.

I arrived early feeling anxiety about the topic and anger that this discussion wasn't on the network news. I sat in an aisle seat so I could stretch my legs, but it didn't matter as the place was almost empty. I could have taken a whole row of seats if that's what I wanted.

The moderator asked the first question: "Are Clones little more than spare parts or do they have rights under our Constitution?"

Reverend Farend began, "Clones are an abomination before God. They are the Devil's work and his creation. We are enduring God's wrath as a result. The misery we experience in our great country saddens me and it does not surprise me that it is Demo-crats that support these wicked laws that allow these beasts to walk amongst us."

Michael from the AFL-CIO said, "We are suffering, Reverend, because sick people have no place to go that they can afford. 74% of American families cannot afford to see a doctor and receive care. Service jobs, technical and good manufacturing jobs have left this country while you focus our attention on school prayer. I can tell you what kids are praying for, Reverend. They are praying for their daddies not to die in war, and they are praying for more food."

The WOLF newsman interrupts, "Wait a minute. I'm not going to listen to you talk about our brave men and women or our great country that way. In the America I live in, we pray for victory because we know our cause is just. We don't mind a little hardship because we know in the end our children will be better off and they will be safe. We are from pioneer stock; we don't waver when the going gets tough. Other countries used to say that Americans were pampered and spoiled but look at us now; we can handle adversity with the best of 'em."

The moderator resumed control. "We are getting away from the question. Dr. Olsen can you help us here?

Dr. Olsen seemed eager to join the discussion. "Yes, of course. Clones are not men; they are a creation of man. They are similar in their DNA to us, like 98% of chimpanzee genes are similar to ours, but they are not human. Clones are a tool for us to use to aid mankind. We will be able to save so many more lives through better organ matching. Instead of animal research that could take decades, research on Clones, because of their similarity to humans, will allow us to develop cures far more effectively. There has been talk of poor treatment of Clones but if you could cure cancer, and it meant only harming a few chimps, wouldn't you do it?"

Reverend Farend responded, "God will not guide us if we think that we are greater that God, our Creator. What good is it if we are healthy but depraved? We see every day in the news that they use the female beasts as harlots. They enter the homes as maids or caretakers for the children. Satan has put this she-beast in your home and she will fulfill any wish commanded of her. Your wife, a good god fearing woman, would be repulsed at these acts. Now the man lives the life of sin and does not share his bed with his wife.

"The homosexuals in Hollywood have several of the male beasts in their home under the guise of being domestics, having sodomy parties and breaking the law. Some are young enough to be children were they not the spawn of Satan.

Reverend Algood spoke for the first time. "I must agree with Reverend Farend on this. Their presence increases sin and furthers disease. They are the fastest growing group of AIDS carriers in the U S. They are being used to commit petty crimes, sometimes as shields, and are being given drugs or alcohol by teenagers just for the thrill of seeing them walk into the street and get hit by cars.

"But what I wanted to address is that the vast majority of Clones are white and they are taking jobs from African-American and Latino workers. They work for almost nothing and look white. Employers want them instead of us. If you are Black and lucky enough to have a job, that dollar you earn is worth a quarter. The dollar just keeps getting weaker and weaker, just like the government's reasons for why there are no jobs. We need to get a dollar from the 1990s and that's what we need to clone!"

Michael of the AFL-CIO had a different take. "You see, that's the problem, Reverend Algood. All Americans are losing jobs--White, Black, and Brown--and we are turning against each other. The fat cats, the politicians and corporations are stacking pies as high as the eye can see and we shake things up hoping it will rain crumbs. Our unions are dying and so are your people. We need to start seeing beyond color. The people who are exploiting us don't care about color. We are all like screws in a machine; we have no humanity. To them we might as well be Clones. They need us only as soldiers, for labor and votes. As they move labor to more profitable locations worldwide they need us less. As they create legislation, appoint judges, staff bureaucracies, consolidate media, change laws making them corporation friendly, they need us less.

"Soon they will not need to go through the charade that they care about America, family, God or you. The wheels will grind automatically and we will all be permanently screwed."

The WOLF newsman said angrily, "This sounds like class warfare nonsense. Americans know that unions are bad for American jobs. That is why unions are going the way of the dinosaur. Reverend Algood has a history of failed liberal causes and I am surprised to hear the Reverend speak to us of morality after what he calls his "indiscretion".

Reverend Algood took offense. "Yes, I was unfaithful to my wife once after a lifetime of doing public service and private good. But it appears to me that the only sin of any consequence to the white right is sex sins. Gays, Abortion, Adultery and Promiscuity, if you created an organization based on your belief, GAAP would be the name. It would identify openings in the body that you and your constituency appear to fear most.

"I do remember however that there were some other sins in the Bible. I remember 'Thou shall not kill' and you keep endorsing, no, blessing wars. I remember 'Thou shall not steal' and you continue to bless the transfer of trillions of dollars from average citizens' Social Security money and tax dollars to defense contractors and corporations.

"What I remember most though was the life of Jesus. He cared for the poor and the sick; he left judgment to his father, in fact asking that he who was without sin throw the first stone at the adulteress.

"He was goodness and love, not hatred and punishment. He despised only the Pharisees, the hypocrites who comprised Israel's religious leaders. They were in cahoots with the money–changers at the temple.

"In Mathew, Jesus addresses them, "Woe to you, teachers of the law and Pharisees, you hypocrites. You are like whitewashed tombs which look beautiful on the outside but on the inside are full of dead men's bones and everything unclean."

The WOLF newsman snickered. "Is this a sermon, Reverend, because certainly there must be one that says, "Thou shall keep thy zipper up."

The moderator then addressed Sara. "Dr. Khan, you have been sitting there quietly. As a Doctor and a Latina woman, you have a unique perspective in this discussion. Is there anything you would like to add to this discussion?"

As interesting and as heated as the discussion was, I was already paying attention to her. Her presence was riveting. She seemed intent on every word that was spoken but unlike the others was not eager to be heard. She appeared the least agitated and the most centered. She was the unknown in this equation and when her tapered hands took the mike, chairs shifted in the audience and heads turned on the panel.

Sara offered her perspective. "Good Morning. I am honored to meet and speak with you today. Public speaking is not something I desire to do. I am not at ease expressing myself in this manner. I wish I had the gift of expression that my fellow panelists have because what I have to say today is vitally important and I need your help.

"Let me begin by saying that I have always had great affection for this country. It was always my mother's dream to become an American.

She and her friends are watching me now and I am sure this makes her happy. Over the last decade many more Mexicans have been allowed to legally enter this country. Unfortunately this happens at a time when there are few jobs available.

"This has led to the type of resentment that immigrants have always faced. We are accused of taking jobs, taking resources away from the society and negatively influencing the culture. This was said of Eastern Europeans in the early 1900s and there were laws banning their immigration. Western European immigrants were also ostracized, lived in ghettos and had high crime rates. They became the Lucky Lucianos, Bugsy Siegels and Vince Mad Dog Coles of the movies we enjoy so much.

"Today we are a nation of Irish, Italian, Jewish immigrants, at first vehemently opposed and now unquestionably American. We hope that the story of immigrant success through hardship will apply to Black and Brown people as well. That is what I would like to share as a Latina woman.

"The story of America that relates to cloning, however, goes deeper into the American psyche. It is the story of American wealth built on stolen land and stolen labor. Native American land allowed a young nation to grow and African slavery allowed it to prosper. America needed to do horrific injustice to both peoples in order to thrive. This required that Americans convince themselves that the Indians were savages and that Africans were chattel. In both cases they were not regarded as human. Otherwise, how could good Christian people hang and whip Blacks and scalp and behead Indians?

"How could we at the most celebrated and enlightened time of our democracy deny Africans constitutional rights with the glorious words of our Declaration of Independence still fresh in our ears? It is simple: dehumanization. We must tell ourselves that the people we are killing are not human."

The panel members were stunned and at first didn't respond. Dr. Khan's remarks had caught everyone by surprise. After the initial shock, there were interruptions, clenched fists, intense looks and waving arms, but she continued.

"Now America is no longer so young but we face a crisis of resources. We have an insurmountable budget deficit, a bottomless pit of a trade deficit, record joblessness, and record foreclosures. Crime has increased and there is a despair I don't think I have ever seen here. Our troops are under attack in three countries. The interest we pay for our debt is strangling us. The lack of health care has led to early deaths, the spread of disease and back door medicine. Without Social Security many of our elderly are dying in the streets.

"Now we seek free labor again. We seek to rip the very hearts of men right out of their bodies in our own self–righteous self-interest. At what cost do we sell our souls, gentlemen, and what is God's retribution for that?"

It was this combination of straight talk, fearlessness and compassion that immediately endeared Sara Khan to me. It was also why she excelled in what remained of the discussion. I waited for her until after the program was over. She was talking with two of the panelists who continued to engage her along with a few members of the audience. I intentionally waited to be the last to talk to her, motioning to others to go ahead of me. It was hard for me to wait because I really wanted to speak with her.

She was energetic and driven but with a softness. Her genuine concern for others was at her core, radiating out. We had coffee and later saw each other once or twice a week. We became very close friends, loving each other's minds and flirting with the idea of expanding our intimacy, but she had to leave the country because of her work and I had to do mine.

We have not seen each other in years. We always try to make the most of our time together but we are not as close as we once were. I hope to recapture some of what we lost when I see her—hopefully today.

Chapter Two

Now as I turn the corner and see Regressive Nature a block away, I feel as eager and as nervous as I did at our first meeting. I stop walking and bend over, resting my hands on my thighs. I exhale deeply. I am exhausted and need to gather my strength. I remain that way, breathing as deeply as I can, staring blankly at the ground. When I think I have consolidated all my strength, I straighten up, wipe the sweat from by face and regain my stride.

As I open the center door to Regressive Nature, the guards immediately notice me. One of them asks for identification and what I am there to buy. I feel like I've been caught speeding and the police suspect the car is stolen. He continues to ask questions while another guard wanders over. People there are well dressed with full pockets. A few of the customers discretely glance over at us as they talk and shop. Others, less affluent, mutter verbal approval of the guard's actions. It seems those closest to poverty resent the poor the most. They seem disappointed when the guards let me pass. Had the guards clubbed me bloody and senseless they would have thought that I somehow deserved it.

As I walk to the back of the store, I hold my head up, ready to make eye contact with anyone who will look at me but no one does. I see a sign towards the back of the store that says: "Meditation classes all day."

As I climb a long narrow flight of stairs, I use the banister for support. At the top of the stairs there is a door on the left that says "Meditation." I turn the knob quietly and open the door slightly so I can peek in. I see about 35 people on mats, many in lotus positions with their eyes closed. I shut the door and turn my attention to the door on the right. It's top half is that thick smoky glass the door is light green. I open it, the room is dark except for one window streaming light through the dust to the hardwood floor. There is another door at the back of the room. I go through, climb another flight of steps and begin to hear footsteps and voices.

The room is large and filled with people waiting to be treated. They are in varying degrees of despair. There is a lady doubled over in pain and moaning as her children console her, one holding her hand and the other patting her back. A couple of large men are standing. They both have grossly infected wounds. They are among the many that can't afford the super-resistant antibiotics and are hoping to find alternative healing methods to fight infection. There is a middle-age man who looks like he has cancer. He is very frail and completely bald except for a few thin, white strands of hair scattered about his head. Without health insurance and government resources, those seeking cures must turn increasingly to non-traditional medicine.

A vain few are seeking special blends that will tighten their skin, assist weight loss and enhance their mood. These blends work well and are sold to high-end customers to finance much of the pro-bono medicine provided here.

Dr. Kahn's Assistants pay huge sums to learn from her. One of her interns is a prominent doctor who wants to add these techniques and ancient secrets to his practice.

The interns once wore white robes to identify themselves but when police raids occurred this made them too easy to identify, so they now wear colored wristbands, which they can discard quickly to blend into the crowd.

I decide to step back and have a seat against the wall in the hallway. I will enter as the crowd begins to thin. I begin to feel a little drowsy and go in and out of sleep for hours. I lift my head and briefly open my eyes as people enter and exit until finally I am completely asleep.

"Hey, you can't stay here." A man is shaking my shoulder and shouting.

I am startled awake and grab him.

"I don't want any trouble but you have to move," he says.

My eyes notice his gray wristband and I release him. "I just need some help," I say.

"Come back tomorrow early and we can help you."

"But I know her."

"She knows everyone," he replies with a slight snicker.

I slide my back up the wall to assist me in getting up. I stumble forward slightly and he jumps back. I remember then that the interns double as security. I've always thought that was a bad idea. These guys are healers not fighters but she is convinced that no one would ever harm her and real guards like the ones downstairs might frighten and alienate her customers. So when I stand up and look down at him from my full height, he seems a little nervous.

"No, I meant that we are friends. Please tell her that Clinton Robeson is here to see her. I'll wait out here in the hall."

He looks relieved and then becomes assertive again. "OK, wait here."

"Come in," the intern says when he returns. "She went to wash up and change."

I go in and take a seat. Several of the interns straighten chairs or complete notes and then leave. Two remain. I recognize one of them from my last visit years ago. He comes over and introduces himself.

"Hi, my name is Tim. We were introduced once awhile back."

"Oh yeah, how you been?" I ask.

"Good, but this looks like more than a social visit."

I tell him I took a bad fall; I leave out the details.

He makes small talk, something I have never been very good at, especially now that my mind is focused elsewhere. I am in danger and have seen so much death recently that I have begun to reflect on things that seemed unimportant before. Mostly I have begun to reflect on the past and whether there is a future beyond my death. I came so close last night! I can still hear the shotgun blast and feel the sting of the shattered glass against my face. One instant: if I had one moment of indecision, would there be only darkness now? The one thing I know for certain is that love is a key to unlocking the mystery of life. Maybe I've solved so few of life's mysteries because I have known so little love in my life.

Yes, I have pursued ideas with intensity; I have enjoyed sex with the joy of a tiger ripping the flesh of its kill, a primitive hunger satisfied. I have had friends, although few, whose company has entertained me, even enriched me. Never have I had a relationship that is somewhat mystical, life-altering or irreplaceable. It makes it difficult to see God in others or in me.

Sara Khan is the only person who sees inside me. When she looks at me, I love the person I see reflected in her eyes. I hope there is a destiny for me where her vision is real.

"I trust if it doesn't rain, she is planning to go to Dr. Benson's party tonight. Do you know Dr. Benson?" the Intern asks.

"Uh no," I reply. "Seems like she has been in there a while."

"Yeah, she is usually done a lot faster. Maybe she's changing for the party."

At that moment she walks in with her arms outstretched. She is smiling and her eyes are sparkling, dancing. She glides toward me. Just the kind of welcome I was hoping for.

She gives me a long hug, tight and affectionate. I try not to wince from the pain in my rib;, I am good at hiding pain. She pulls back, grabs both my hands and says, "Let me look at you." When she does, her eyes lose their glow. Instantly she sees my needs and I become a patient. She notices my clothes, neat but shabby and wreaking of poverty. She motions to one of her Interns as she says to me, "You poor thing, we're going to fix you right up. You have a party to go to."

After Sara cares for my wounds we do some quick shopping, and board a plane to D.C. I have new clothes, relief from pain and the perfect companion by my side. It is a short flight and a slighter longer ride from the airport to our destination.

We approach a grey sprawling mansion and drive up its long circular driveway. The party is much as she has described it: A gathering of Washington's wealthy political elite and a lot of old money. I can tell the new money people because they are trying too hard and talking too loud.

There are a few from think tanks, the military and the media. One media mogul brought a news anchor and the Defense Industry guy brought a general; everyone treats them like show dogs. There are only a few people there who look like they belonged there less than we do. They are Security people trying to blend in.

The place is huge. The marble floors are laid in intricate patterns, complex and hypnotic. I find myself staring and quickly stop so as not to draw attention to us. I look around more casually and notice several paintings in frames that are as unique as the paintings themselves. All appear to be from the Impressionist era, so I look for a Van Gogh--my favorite—but I am disappointed.

The painting style changes to Modern as we move closer to the Great Room, a style that evokes energy and curiosity. The chandeliers are dazzling arrays of light angled through finely cut glass. I feel like I am in ancient Rome awaiting Caesar.

Instead, in walks the Kingmaker, Prescott Thysen, the party's guest of honor. Thysen was the chief architect of the former President's many victories.

Dr. Benson is appropriately flattering and everyone begins to applaud.

"What are we doing here?" I wonder out loud.

"I thought you might enjoy this," Sara says. "There are some interesting people here."

"No, Sara, I meant how did you get invited to something like this? These people don't represent your politics or your class."

The applause continues. She laughs, "Do you know Senator Townsend? Well, he's my Dad."

"WHAT?" I ask in astonishment.

I scan her face for some sign that she is joking. The applause dies down. We move away looking for a place where we can talk privately. I want to talk outside, so I look for an exit. It is only then that I notice that the largest and most beautiful room I have ever seen has no windows.

She nods at one of the poorly disguised security men. We leave the Great Room and go to an ante-chamber to talk privately. "I know you are surprised and probably a little disappointed that I never mentioned this before," Sara says.

More than a little, I thought. Outloud I say, "Well, I am surprised. We were so close, I thought that . . ."

She stops me. "Clint, there are things about me no one knows but you. You are very important to me but I needed to keep this secret. Now I will share even this with you."

"OK, I'm listening."

"I told you all about me and my Mom and not knowing my father for so many years and that empty space, all those feelings. Everyone thought I was so pretty, I got great grades, I worked hard, and I was thoughtful and caring. Why didn't my father want me? I had grandparents who would rather pay us than to admit that I existed."

Her eyes fill with tears but instead she smiles. "You know how stubborn I can be. I couldn't accept that. I forced a meeting my first year in college. It was not hard to find him; he was already a Congressman. I was prepared to threaten to go to the newspapers if he did not see me but once he saw me he melted. Here was this guy looking like a comic-book hero, strong, confident, poised. I simply walked up to him and said in my thickest Mexican accent, 'Senor, I am your daughter Carmen.'

"He looked at me for a moment and then his body went suddenly rigid. He held me and collapsed on his knees and sobbed, 'I'm sorry, I'm sorry' over and over again. When I finally pulled him up we talked for hours. Over the years I found that he is a great guy, he just wasn't a great father. We have developed a wonderful relationship and most of the hurt is gone. The hardest part of the love I have for him is the hurt he caused my mother. She will never forgive him, or so she says."

"Why did you never mention him"? I ask.

"Just because of politics," Sara replies. "His enemies could destroy him with this information. They could question his morality with a family out of wedlock and his character for withholding this information. He said he would go public if I wanted him to. He even told his wife and sons about me. I was the one who said no. It would have been the perfect revenge. I would have received acknowledgement as his daughter so long denied me, but as I said I had grown to love him."

"What about your mother? I'm sure she doesn't love him. Why doesn't she expose him?"

Sara smiles. "I'm not sure she ever loved any other man."

"What about your stepfather?" I ask.

"Well, he really loves her and I'm sure she loves that. She can manage him and she can manage her emotions around him. If you have crazy passionate love, that's all there is. Nothing is more nourishing or more giving. It is like the liquid in the womb. When that person leaves you it is like being at the bottom of a waterfall. You are helpless, drowning, tossed about and pounded again and again.

"Nothing can match the sheer intensity of those feelings except the joy of knowing you will never have to experience them again. My stepfather's devotion insures that she never will. She is content, sometimes happy, except for when someone talks about my father. She fears what he represents but loves him for having shown her the edge of her emotional limits."

"Wow."

I love Sara's mind and her intuition. I know at this moment that she is the one to teach me the meaning of love. This woman, part temptress and part Dali Lama, will be my guide to self-discovery. As I gaze at her in admiration, my eyes linger just a little too long.

She grabs my hand. "Come, let me introduce you to my father."

By now many of the guests are milling about holding cocktails or *hors d'oeuvres*. Others are moving from group to group like insurance salesmen. Sara leads me to an L-shaped room where the host Dr. Benson, her father and three guests are chatting. One of the guests is the only Black man at the gathering. I recognize him from the news as Norman Oliver Sewell, selected as an Economic Advisor by the President. This is a high profile position and although he does not have to be confirmed by the Senate, the President wants him displayed.

All administrations now routinely have African Americans and Latinos as part of their Cabinet. Few are actually in their inner circle. N.O.Sewell, a brilliant economist, is an exception. He and the President are close personal friends. The other guests in the room are the media mogul and his anchorman. The two are sitting together, although I can't see whether there is a leash or not.

"Hello, Senator and Dr. Benson, this is Clint."

"Sara," says her father, beaming. "I'm so glad you made it."

"Good to see you, young lady." They both hug her and introduce her to the others in the room. He stands next to her and on the pretext of making her a drink they move away from the others and talk privately. I sit down.

They are coaching Sewell. The Anchor, Shill O'Reely of Wolf News, is feeding him verbatim the questions he can expect on next week's interview, including good responses to the "hard-hitting" questions. Senator Benson also adds his insights. I might as well be a pillow on the couch for all the attention they have paid to me after the initial kind greeting.

After covering the prep session questions, they move to the final question, which will be initiated by O'Reely. He wants the question to be: "Do you feel you are living the American Dream?"

Sewell starts to reply when the Mogul stops him.

"Gents, lets make the whole interview about the American Dream. We can use bold graphics in the background and display the flag, pictures of immigrants at Ellis Island, and that sort of stuff."

Sewell is concerned. "You're the expert, but I think what we had was the basis for a real good interview. Shill's questions allow me to explain the strengths of our economic plan in a way that will give hope to those in need."

"We have no greater strength than the American Dream," The Mogul continues. "It keeps 90% of all wealth in the hands of 10% of the people. It keeps CEO's in our great land making 1100 times what workers earn. It means we can take hundreds of billions out of their retirement funds and use it to make us more money and they will wave flags while we do it. We give them fewer services, less power, less respect and when they go bankrupt they blame themselves because, as you know, everyone can make it in America. When they don't blame themselves, they blame Negros, Clones or illegal aliens. No offense."

Sewell ignores the no offense comment. "I understand that we have to promote values but I'm just saying lets give them some facts as well."

The Mogul looks at Dr. Benson who gives him a subtle nod. He then says, "The values are the facts."

At this moment the Kingmaker walks in, everyone greets him and Sara and her father Senator Townsend return to the conversation. "Don't let me interrupt; looks like you were on a roll." He laughs, "I was just explaining to Norman here that values are facts. Look, this country has been losing more jobs than it makes since the millennium began; we have created so much debt that taxpayers, the poor and the middle-class pay $100 billion a year in new taxes created by the debt. The size of government has increased by almost 10% each year; mass layoffs occur if companies make 1% less profit than they did last year. It's true that the nation's GNP has grown but not the salaries of the average person. Those are facts.

"Here are some more facts. Corporations don't want to hire American workers because they cost too much. We don't have to have any allegiance to them or America. In an all-volunteer Army, wealthy children don't fight in America's wars. We have record defense spending every year, yet the troops have to fight to get body armor and armor for their vehicles. The annual Defense budget is up to $700 Billion a year, none of it for Homeland Security it has its own budget. None of it is for the wars. That comes from the Supplemental, now up to $300 billion a year. So why are we giving Defense contractors three quarters of a trillion dollars that is not for domestic security or fighting wars? People don't know and they don't care.

Dr. Benson jumps into the conversation and says, "Now let me give you my vision of America."

They laugh in unison; Sara and I exchange a glance.

He continues, "We are at war. We are at war against the enemy within. Like a cancer they eat away our great democracy. They hate America and they hate freedom. They don't support our troops and give comfort to the enemy. They blame America for all their problems and expect government to fix them.

"They don't know what hard work and sacrifice is, do they? They don't know why we have flags on our cars and God in our hearts. They want you to live in a world of abortion, gay marriage, sex and rap music. That's the Hollywood America. Well, the America I represent is the Heartland. The blood that makes that heart beat is the blood of patriots. It flows to every part of our nation where liberty is loved. We will spread this good blood until we are cleansed of our enemies, foreign and domestic. We will remain strong and determined, clear in what we believe in and what we stand for. God bless America."

He pretends to wipe a tear from his eye. They applaud and laugh. Norman gets it; he's laughing too.

I can tell Sara is steaming but she conceals it well and asks a gentle and probing question with a forced smile. "Aren't you afraid that the people will catch on?"

"Catch on to what, my dear? We haven't given them lies; we have just said that we share their values, their hopes and their dreams."

Looking down at her drink, stirring and staring at it she says, "But you don't."

"Yes, that's true, but for a long time there was a large group of Americans that felt that government betrayed them. Government gave Blacks rights in the south and took them from southerners, government pulled out of Viet Nam, almost agreeing with those who said the soldiers were baby killers. Kennedy betrayed the Cubans with Bay of Pigs. The government was taxing everyone to pay for these expensive programs to help people they did not consider worth the expense. Roe v Wade and the pill took power from men at home and in the workplace. The average white male felt like he was paying for this chaos with his money. Simply put, he was losing power. He hated the media and seemed to be hated by it. The media promoted civil rights, hated the war, loved warrior women and gun control.

"We gave them a government that voices their values, so we can do no wrong. We also have Wolf news that gives them the values they want to hear. They have been looking for an alternative for a long time. As long as they know we won't desert them, that we will stick to our guns, they will support us with an incredible passion."

"So," she says sarcastically, "they've won."

"It would appear." The Mogul smiles.

There is so much I want to say but I must remain inconspicuous. From the moment I walked in I have tried not to think of the risks I am taking. Government law prohibits only one type of cloning. It is colloquially called the Master Race Amendment. It prohibits research for the purpose of creating idealized humans by using genes of various donors.

The Defense Dept. started a program that preceded the law for "strategic military purposes." The program was an overwhelming failure. Of hundreds only 50 of us lived. Only 30 of us were usable for the purpose intended. Since the project was so secret we were taken into the families of top-level operatives where we were presented as adopted children. We made many trips to "Daddy's" job where the experiments and training continued. That was my family in Virginia.

Only half of us remain now. Suicide and suicide missions are the reasons. There are others in hiding like me. I know that by now I am being checked out by security, but without fingerprints or an eye scan they will find it difficult to positively ID me.

I'm also guessing that since this project remains so hush-hush, my image won't come up when sent to the FBI and other agencies. Yet it is probably wise not to attract attention to myself. I'll just play the dumb boyfriend or date or whatever I'm supposed to be.

"You haven't said much. Are we boring you?" Shill O'Reely inquires.

Oh great, I think, *he's playing journalist.* "No, just soaking it all in," I reply.

Sara gives me a look and then looks at her father.

Dr. Benson says, "What's wrong, Sara? You're pretty quiet today. I like to sharpen my wit on the dull rock of your beliefs. Are you being reserved because of your gentleman friend? I'm sorry, son, what was your name again."

"It's Clint, Dr. Benson."

"Clint, you would not think less of Miss Sara here if she spoke her mind, would you?"

"No, she has a wonderful mind."

"Good, good, and seeing that you admire her thinking so much, I'm sure that being a gentleman you would not let her defend those ideas all by herself, would you?"

"With all due respect, sir, there are only six of you. She does not need any help."

They laugh.

Senator Townsend, who enjoyed the compliment, is still smiling when he says, "Don't include me with them."

This gets a response from Drydock, the mogul. "Ah, the opposition speaks. Somebody tape him, please. They're a quickly vanishing species, almost extinct. Quiet, everybody, as we tape the call of a yellow-tailed liberwill."

They laugh again.

"Thanks for the gracious introduction. Yes, I am a rare bird and you guys are like pigeons shitting on everything we built."

He begins his response to equal laughter.

"What was conveniently left out of that eloquent presentation of civics was the bait and switch that occurred when these disgruntled Americans came to collect their prize. You promised an end to abortion and to put Gays and Blacks in their place, to make them safe and pure, so they vote for you. You gave them little victories and big rhetoric while you robbed them blind. Let's go back in history to your real birth, not born again rhetoric.

"For this we have to go back to the Great Depression. You remember, the top 1% owned 42% of the wealth in the country and their share kept increasing. Remember the Revenue Act of 1926, which gave a two-thirds tax cut to anyone earning over $1,000,000 a year. Production was great and corporate profits were up 65% but workers' income was up only 8%. Not enough people to buy all these products. So you guys decided to come up with Credit. You, the guys who are always talking about values, changed the consumer mindset from pay as you go through self-sacrifice to the buy on credit mindset we have now because of your greed.

"You needed people to buy all the cars, appliances, gadgets and gimmicks being overproduced in the 20s, so you gave us Buy now, Pay later and changed America forever.

"Then when the unregulated banks ran out of money, they foreclosed on American homes and businesses. President Hoover blamed the people for lacking character, self-reliance and independence. You gave us the Depression. No government aid. As a result your party did not hold a majority in Congress until 1980s.

"It's like they say, the past is prelude. As early as 2004 the top 1% owned 40% of all household wealth and received more pretax income than the bottom 40%. Huge tax cuts are being given to the rich; the laws and safeguards put into place after the Depression to protect people from business gone amok, you call regulation.

"We have record foreclosures and record bankruptcies because credit is out of control. Unions are weak and our nation and its citizens are in tremendous debt but you won't change course; instead you go faster and harder. You're like a car that is headed towards a cliff that is out of sight but that you know is there. You cut the brake line and floor it because you enjoy the ride so much. Tell me, do you know something I don't know?"

The Kingmaker clears his throat and the room falls silent. He sips some water before speaking and the room remains quiet enough to hear him swallow. He speaks.

"Yes, the American people like a good story. We like to feel strong, independent and moral, especially if it makes us feel we are better than the other guy. It's our competitive upbringing. We are cowboys, pioneers and patriots who came to this great land for religious freedom. We are just in war. We are richer than others because of our hard work and our goodness. Our enemies are jealous of our way of life.

"The truth is that there is a dark side to this country. Slavery accounted for much of our income. We stole land from Indians and nearly eliminated them. Our wealth was built on the exploitation of child labor and workers without any rights. Our agri-business is built at the expense of hardworking farmers, our railroads through the blood of Chinese immigrants. We have profited from wars and made war for profit. We will exploit culture, religion or race and we have no remorse. There will always be a dark side to wealth. I embrace it.

"We have gone into outer space, conquered all enemies and created more assets than any civilization known to man. To be an American is to be envied or feared across the globe. This could not have occurred without the very essence of darkness. It could not have occurred without the sacrifice of the ignorant many for the sacred and gifted few. Doesn't our brain exist only for the 10% we use? Doesn't life itself exist for those few meaningful moments? Hasn't it been that way since the days of the great pharaohs and pyramids? Hundreds of bees work to serve the Queen. If they are loyal, then they survive and prosper.

"Americans know these truths but they don't want to accept them. They want myths and Rambo Movies. They want flags, not responsibility. No one wants guilt; everyone wants riches. We chosen few are America's mind and we will lead them to the devils work in Jesus' name.

"But do not despair, you do have a place in all this. Our overindulgence is addictive and for the good of the body and the head there are rare occasions when we must be stopped because we cannot do it. It is not in our nature. That is when genuine religious concepts, true democratic ideals and honest journalism act as a vaccine. They restore order and we are ready to resume. The mistake of people like you is that you want to keep injecting your serum into us until you kill us. Small well-timed doses are what America wants from you, nothing more."

I can't take it anymore. "So, are Clones to be the next dark sacrifice for American greatness?" I ask.

I turn red, and my hands are clenched and rigid. I know I have to loosen up but I am seething with anger.

Sara, who is now sitting next to me, opens my hand and holds it.

"Yes," says the Kingmaker, "they are."

I can tell from the Kingmaker's speech that he has seen Sara's appearance on C-SPAN. Had he just been watching that day? No, more likely it meant that he had arranged to have her investigated. Anger and anxiety wrestle in my belly as I selfishly wonder if they know my identity. The Kingmaker continues to talk as he puts his cigarette out. I look at the crushed and bent butt, only half used. Would he end my life as casually? Hidden under his veneer of civility is a visceral evil that makes my skin crawl. This evil cleverly makes good men enablers of their own misfortune. The Kingmaker is a wordsmith, pounding through repetition, ideas forged in hell.

I turn and look into Sara's mystical eyes. I have found the meaning of love and the meaning of evil here today. Like trains headed toward each other at full speed, the embodiment of these ideals smile politely at each other across a room, a room with no windows.

I lean over and whisper to Sara, "I need to leave."

Sara goes over to inform her Dad. He looks disappointed and then angry. He waves at me and smiles thinly. Sara hugs him and starts towards me. As I grab her arm I am keenly aware of the Security personnel and make sweeping glances around the room.

She feels the tension in my body and asks, "Are you OK?"

I nod. I can't talk right now, not even to her. In fact I am angry with her, angry that she is somehow part of them. I am also mad at myself for not fighting back. I am mad at myself for grinning and acting like a slave, so I choose to impose my manhood upon the one I love rather than acknowledge my impotence in combating my enemy.

"How can you listen to that crap?"

She looks at me with understanding. "I know it must have been difficult for you."

"Just me?"

"No, especially you. You know how I think and you know my heart. I think what was said was cruel and ugly but I did not need to respond for you to know how I feel and it would not have changed their minds one bit. As it turns out we learned something about them and they learned very little about us. This is the best conversation you can have with an enemy."

"I'm not so sure they know so little about us. Do you think we were investigated?"

"Clint, no one knew you were coming. You did not even know. Yes, they check all uninvited guests but from what you told me, only the Defense Dept at the highest levels knows about you. That shouldn't come up on a routine search. As for me, yes, they know all about me. They know I am a doctor that sometimes uses banned healing methods. They know my general political views, but I am no threat so I am safe."

A limo is waiting for us. Once we pull away from the house, I feel relieved. Sara starts being playful and my anger dissipates. We laugh and touch, departing to a playful part of us, devoid of reason or maturity. I suggest we go for a walk in downtown Washington. I want to hold her hand, enjoy the connection, the energy of attraction pulsating up our spines, alive in this innocent, symbolic joining.

She looks deep into my eyes, strokes my hand and says, "No walk, you need to save your strength."

"It's ok, I feel fine," I say, giving a hearty tap to my bandaged ribs thinking that she is still concerned about my injuries.

She smiles and shakes her head. "I hope so," she says, "because you're not too bright. Driver, take us to the Clairmont Hotel."

Apparently she has more than symbolism on her mind.

We begin to kiss, more and more passionately. Her neck is long and elegant; my tongue glides down its length as excited as a kid on a roller coaster. I grab her waist and lift her onto my lap. She looks startled and then her eyelids lower assuming a primitive trance-like state. Her skin is beautiful, not unmarked, but etched with the distinct marking of a tomboy past. Her hips begin subtle movements, and the hands that moments earlier gently caressed, now claw and crave. Her hair is everywhere like the fur of passion.

I feel as if blood is rushing to every part of my body, every vein, nerve and muscle. I am like a sports car that has gone from 0-60 and now suddenly has to brake. I am a passionate lover not a skilled one. I know what a woman needs but my needs consume me. Once hard, I will charge at a firing squad if pussy lies behind it. My stamina and desire give some women pleasure, those who like honest passion. For those who do not, I know that I can be frightening.

She is easily the most beautiful woman I have ever been with and the most important to me. I don't want to scare her away. I won't try to fuck her in the car; she would never forgive me. She feels like she wants it too but the driver is here. The window separates us from him and is darkly tinted. Maybe I should try. I lift her dress so I can feel her thighs around me, the wetness of her panties, the heat and the smell of sex. I start to move my hand to her inner thigh; she shifts her hips but sends a cautionary hand to meet mine.

"How far are we from the hotel?" she whispers.

I look around but do not recognize anything. I activate the speaker. "Driver, are we almost there?"

"Yes sir, I'm taking a short cut. We should be there in 10 minutes."

She looks at me, gives me a soft kiss on my lips and then dismounts, returning to the seat beside me. "Put your arm around me," she says and then closes her eyes.

I put my arms around her and look at my watch. I'm sure he can get us there in eight minutes if he drives a little faster.

I am just about to ask him to speed up when the speaker comes on. "Sir, the car seems to be overheating. I just need to add some water. I will pull over to the side of the road."

Great, Don't these guys do maintenance checks? This could add another ten minutes.

As we leave the road, the crackling sound of gravel awakens Sara. I start to explain our delay, but when she looks around she looks back at me and says, "Clint, we are no where near the Clairemont." She taps on the window. "Driver?"

The tinted glass slowly lowers. We see the driver's cap, his face and then a gun. "Get out," he says and shakes the gun toward the door he wants us to use to exit. Three men with bigger guns emerge from the woods at the side of the road. Near the men, mostly shaded by trees and the darkness, are two black Hummers. I look around. There is no way to escape without endangering Sara.

I appeal to the driver. "Let her go," I say and I plead with my eyes.

He says, "She won't be hurt."

Our arms and mouths are taped quickly and professionally and we are walked to the vehicles. We receive injections. I experience euphoria and then emptiness. The black Hummers resume their journey under cover of darkness of the night sky.

Chapter Three

Norman Oliver Sewell is scheduled to appear on Wolf News. His mother, Betty, has invited several of her friends over to watch the broadcast and has prepared a meal for everyone. He is by far the most successful of all the kids from the old neighborhood and of course this means that she was the best parent. Betty is nearly bursting with pride. It's important not to brag though. She has to wait for someone else to say something good about her son and then pretend not to care all that much. Words ache to leave her mouth.

He will be working directly with the President, earning a huge salary and doing something important for the country, yet Betty's friends talk about everything but him. If she didn't know better she'd swear they were doing it on purpose.

Greta just keeps going on and on about her Gout. Put down the shrimp, Greta. When food begins to hurt you and you still eat it, it's time to wave goodbye, put 'em in a bottle and send them back to sea.

Now they're talking about the trip up here and the drive. Its only 30 miles from the old neighborhood but you'd think they were Lewis and Clark, mapping trails in the wilderness and shooting wild beasts.

"Want some more snacks, or do y'all want to wait for the show? I think it's on in about 15 minutes."

Greta says, "I was hoping the real food would be out by then." They laugh and start talking about food.

Now that's why that child is so fat. Betty has given Greta the perfect opening to talk about her baby and all she can think to say is, 'Where is the rest of the food?'

Betty hears a key opening the front door, and her husband rushes in.

"Where have you been, Honey? You know, you almost missed him!"

"Hi, ladies. Betty, you know you turn on that electric collar you make me wear if I'm not back home on time."

Everyone laughs.

"How was your trip up here, ladies?"

The look he gets from his wife lets him know that was the wrong question to ask. He thinks for a moment, looks at her and then over fifty years of marriage tells him what's in her heart. When one of the ladies takes a pausing breath, he interjects, "So, village, what do you think of our child"?

"He always was smart but I didn't think he would go this far," Thelma says.

"Most kids are smart but he was always trying to learn something new," another friend mentions.

They start discussing Norman as if they might discover that one distinguishing feature they could pass on to help their grandkids succeed. Magically, they all could then work for the President one day.

Greta joins in. "One thing we know for sure: He had pretty average parents."

She looks at Norman's mom, waits for her eyes to meet hers and they all burst out laughing, Betty included. While still smiling she turns the TV on. They watch intently feeling joy and pride in Norman's accomplishments. They are all elated by the experience.

Thelma's son Walter and his friends are also gathered but at a different place and for a different purpose.

"Turn the game on man; nobody wants to hear this," Walter shouts. "Don't you want to hear Norm? He's on Wolf." Walter rejoins everybody in the living room.

"I thought it was the Home Shopping Network, since Norm always sells out."

"Oooh, that's kinda rough."

"Well, almost everybody I know has it rough, but all he and his crew are dealing is fear and smear. They use Black people and anybody else they can to scare people: Clones, Immigrants, Liberals, Gays, Terrorists, Muslims, the French. They scare us and then tell us they must spy on us to protect us. They take all our tax money to fund wars and tax cuts, take away rights and then smear anybody that interferes with their right to do it, even their own buddies. Look where we are now; America is in deep trouble."

Slim says "Do you mean look at where *you* are now? For some of us life hasn't changed all that much in the last ten years. We didn't have nothing then and we don't have nothing now. It's you brothers that had all that rich shit who are sweating now. Boohoo, they took all my shit. I aint got my Lexus; I got to drive a Ford. Boohoo, I got to watch TV with you broke Negroes instead of my big screen plasma. Oh, will I ever get head from white women again?"

Most of them laugh.

"Walt, all them're the same to me--Governors, Mayors, Conservative, Liberal, Black, White--none of them never did a damn thing for me."

"Slim, I don't remember you complaining about watching my big ass TV. In fact your no beer-bringing ass would always be in my favorite seat. As for white girls, I still got your Daddy."

More laughter.

"Yo, you Negroes are regressing. I came to watch the game but I guess we can watch Norm for five minutes. We did grow up with the brother, and Walt, you were his best friend and best man. I'm surprised at you."

"That's best man from the first marriage when the brother was still sane. I know that as we earn degrees, travel and get large, we seek out new things, challenge some of those old ideas and values, but the man has no center. It's like he rejects everything Black. African Art is not real art; Black plays that make it to Broadway are 'cornbread'; Black women are 'too confrontational' and the 'race' has been conditioned to avoid blame and accept handouts. This brother hasn't just lost his way, he's lost."

"Yeah, that sounds pretty bad, but I still say when things were going good, the only time we would see half of you rich Negroes was when you had to go to the barber or to church. Even if you had some pussy on the side you made her come downtown to meet you. At least he was honest; He didn't want to see y'all or nobody that looks like y'all. He moved his family out so he wouldn't have no reason to come here. His head looks all jacked-up though 'cause he can't find no decent barber where he lives. I know he can't get the Holy Ghost at that church he goes to, although it looks like the barber got the Holy Ghost while he was cutting his hair. Brother looks like Don King."

"On the real though, Slim, its hard out there. There's so few principled brothers in the workplace. You bring up unity and they look at you like you're a dinosaur. Most of us are just out for ourselves and trying to survive. Most of the young boys don't know anything about their history and don't want to know; they just want to get paid. They never saw their parents struggle the way we saw our parents struggle: doing hard labor jobs, stuffed in small apartments, drugs and crime all around them. They came up in the suburbs, decent home, nice car, fewer kids, older, educated and more affluent parents. They never saw hardship.

"We are losing our history and our culture. When we were young there were books by Ralph Ellison, Richard Wright, James Baldwin. We had sports heroes that raised their fists during the Olympic Games; we had Muhammad Ali. James Brown sang, 'I'm Black and I'm Proud.' Our churches preached for the struggle, and we wore dashikis and Afro hair styles as our fashion statement. What culture do we have now? Rap, Rap videos and sit-coms"?

"He's on."

"Hey, he looks good, he stayed in shape."

"Yeah, it's all those cucumber sandwiches."

"You know Rap ain't that bad."

"Shhh, can I hear this?"

Norman Oliver Sewell has just completed the interview, which was recorded days earlier. He is watching the interview on his laptop. He is flying in on the one full-service carrier left in America and he is flying first class. He has a style that is elegant and old money conservative. His economics may be neo-conservative but not his look. Nothing about him says dirt farmer twice removed.

As the plane began its descent, his spirits followed. He loved his parents but sometimes felt embarrassed by them. His father gave him a work ethic and solid values and his mother made her children the absolute priority of her life. They did everything right but they just did it with too much flair. Like Magic Johnson they had mastered the fundamentals but had to make the fancy pass.

Both were gregarious and charismatic. His father was a man's man who women are attracted to and men liked to be around. His house is where the neighborhood men met and watched the games and the fights. It was where the extended family had the barbecues.

During childhood, his mother was head of the PTA and became President of the local school board. He was expected to be a role model for the other children and he blamed his mother for not having much fun as a kid. In truth, Norm recognized that he just never had as much personality as his parents did. So he spent more and more time on academics, ruining any chance of being cool or being appreciated by most school-age girls.

He always had friends; it was impossible not to, given who his parents were. But he always liked the conversations he had in his head better.

While growing up, reality was shallow, fast paced and irrational. Its primary purpose seemed to be to escape boredom at any cost. He wasn't bored as a child because he was interested in a variety of things. Maybe he had shut himself out of all the fun things, so he has had to develop other interests. Whatever. He hated the emotions and insecurity he felt. He hated going home.

Norm's mom mentioned to him that she had invited her friends and invited Walt and others to greet him at the house. *She is still making play dates for me.* Norm chuckles. He reasoned that if he can maneuver his way through boring cocktail parties and political functions he can get through this. Although when he was working it was like he was acting; with his parents he is transported back to a time when he was vulnerable and insecure and being around them made him acknowledge weaknesses that might still be present in him.

Norm's friend Walt was a good guy, Norm acknowledged. Always popular and smart, he would have been the most successful of them, if not for Norm's success. He used to look out for Norm and was smart enough to understand what he was going through and give advice. He also would gently intervene when the guys were teasing him. Norm could fight pretty well but because of Walt he didn't have to fight as much.

Walt went to Howard and then Columbia University. He was Student Government President at Howard and fought against apartheid and for prisoner rights. At Columbia he studied law and through a couple of chance meetings ended up representing many athletes and rappers as an agent. He met his wife, an aspiring singer, while working with a client. It turns out she liked being a mother more than being a singer. She just liked being around famous people and Walt's job provided plenty of contact with them. They were living the American Dream until one day he and Cody, one of their friends from high school, were riding from the old neighborhood to Walt's house.

Walt was driving his Jag convertible and the police pulled them over. Walt had witnessed brutal examples of police abuse as a teenager and in political protests and demonstrations. Now he was more used to seeing police as public servants who always treated him with respect and on a couple of occasions gave him warnings instead of speeding tickets when he deserved them. So the instant hostility of this policeman took him by surprise. He was loud, mean and derisive and tried very hard to provoke Walt.

It was difficult, but Walt remained calm. He asked for Cody's I D; Cody protested stating that he was not driving. The cop insisted and threatened to arrest him if he did not provide it. The policeman went back to his car forcing them to remain seated for about twenty minutes. Two other police cars pulled up behind them, lights flashing. They talked briefly and then approached the car on both sides, guns drawn.

Cody had an outstanding warrant. Because he moved or said something they didn't like, they beat Cody to death on the side of the road as Walt watched, his cheek forced against the pavement by a policeman's knee.

Walt did everything he could to bring these killer-cops to justice. He got the best criminal attorneys he knew, he called or wrote anyone he thought could help and he spent loads of money. It didn't make a difference. They walked. So did his business clients, some because he neglected them and others because they felt he was now too controversial.

He decided to go into criminal law. Because of his name recognition he got a few high profile clients and of course rappers and athletes who ran afoul of the law. But life was never again like it was before. He did a lot of pro bono work and formed People Organized in Response to Killing. When the economy left so many without jobs, he worked to help people keep their homes and savings, almost impossible with the new bankruptcy and foreclosure laws. His wife stayed, which surprised Norm, but she aged noticeably, almost overnight it seemed.

Over the years it became harder for Norm to talk to Walt. Norm felt that Walt had changed. Where there used to be a sparkle, now there was an edge. Walt, on the other hand, thought that Norm was a big sellout. If it weren't for those damn cops, he'd be out in Larchmont, donating to the UNCF and enjoying his tax cut, Norm thought.

Norm hopes Reverend Toliver will be there at the house. He's someone who understood that racism was no longer the problem that suppressed Blacks. He knew that a good spiritual foundation, concerned parenting and individual achievement were the way to overcome poverty and ignorance.

In the past, Toliver was one of those poverty preachers who blamed everything on the white man. Now, with funding from Faith-Based Initiatives, he has transformed his storefront church into a Cathedral. His church offered job training for the indigent in the community. They trained the poor to be Nurses Aides and Home Health Care workers for the elderly .They provided the buses to take them to the affluent communities where they worked. They also provided a juvenile residence program for homeless teenage felons. They could use the church address for house arrest purposes, relieving the overcrowded jails.

To decrease the 70% minority dropout rate, his church participated in the special voucher program, which allowed at risk students to join the Army to earn their high school diploma. The program required one year of military service for each year of high school missed. The voucher program has grown since the standards for G.E.D.'s were raised to meet national standards for high schools.

Rererend Toliver also provided an adoption agency for pregnant women and teens who would otherwise go to jail for having abortions. The adopters paid the church for the babies and the women received 10%. If an adoptive family cannot be found, the young mothers are sent to the Christian Light orphanages where the children develop a strong work ethic by working for the state.

Yes, Rev. Toliver realized that social justice and struggles for equality were antiquated solutions. Jesus wanted him to fight against gay marriage and stop abortion and bless those who fight for freedom. If we love our country and our god, blessings will continue to flow.

"Boy, pass that macaroni and cheese over here. You act like you're afraid you won't get it back."

"I was going to ask him if he needed parking lights for that bowl."

"Yeah, it's just like when he was little, making a little food fortress of the things he likes."

"Are you going to do that at them state dinners you go to, Norm?"

"Yeah, are you going to be like: 'Excuse me, Mr. Ambassador, but you need to step back from the biscuits'."

Norman smiles.

Slim says, "You know how much money I could get if I took a picture of you with a hamhock in your mouth and sold it to the newspapers. So why don't you just save me the trouble and break me off some dollars right now?"

"Slim, you know I don't cook any hamhocks in my greens," says Betty, joining in.

. "I use smoked turkey. And besides, my baby is a sophisticated man now. He can't be seen eating no hamhocks." She then whispers audibly to Norm, "So I put them in some aluminum foil and stuck them in your briefcase."

Everyone laughs.

"Reverend, we haven't heard from you since the blessing. Is the food that good?"

He chews a little faster while they laugh. "Betty, you know I'm a man of the cloth so I don't make religious jokes, but this food is so good it almost got me speaking in tongues. I haven't said nothing yet 'cause I'm afraid of what might come out. Slim, we ever gonna get you back down to the church?"

"Reverend, that place is so big I might hear an echo and think God is calling me," Slim replied.

The Reverend looks at him seriously and says, "Maybe he is."

Slim gives Reverend Toliver a half smile and then whispers to Walt, "Not with those jobs wiping rich people's asses, he's not."

The Reverend looks at them and Slim flashes a full plastic smile at Reverend Toliver.

Everyone broke up into smaller groups after dinner. Slim and Walt were talking out on the porch when Norm opened the front door to walk the Reverend to his car.

"Got far to go Reverend?" Walt asks.

"Going out to Larchmont. Your mother tells me it's not far from where you used to live."

That stung. Walt knew that Toliver didn't intend to hurt him but he did, so he responded, "Possibly, Reverend, but I'm sure we took different roads to get there."

"I don't know what you mean, Walter."

"I mean that at one time you had bigger dreams that didn't include a bigger house."

"I serve God in the biggest house of all and that's true regardless of where I live."

Slim spoke up. "My boy read you right, Reverend. Years ago you wanted to serve mankind; now you want to be a 'Master of the Universe'. Preachers tell us now that Jesus hates. He mostly hates the homos, terrorists and liberals. When I was growing up, a Preacher helped you through your misery, shared what little he had and spoke of Jesus in a way that made you want to love him too. No, I ain't turning the other cheek or giving up the coat off my back, but you knew he would. He reached your soul and made you want to be a better person. It was about helping those who needed help and doing the right thing. It was about love. Where's the love, Reverend?"

"Slim's right. I think about all those people years ago rushing to see the 'Passion', crying about how Jesus suffered for us instead of why he suffered. The religious leaders of his time had sold out to the moneychangers corrupting the church for cash. They were more interested in their own power than the people. The people were not blameless either. They chose the warrior Barabbas over Jesus, which meant Jesus had to die. Today we continue to choose Barabbas over

Jesus in our hearts, choosing the path of fear and violence over love and justice. Today we love Barabbas and call him Jesus.

"Preachers today bless the policies that keep us at war and reinforce fear and prejudice. They stand silent as programs that sustain the poor, children and old people are killed. They hold their government to no moral standard.

Rev. Toliver responded "Look, I have to get home but I want to remind you that Jesus said, 'Go and sin no more' not just do anything you feel like. There was a time before the Civil Rights struggles when the main thing we had to fight against was government: its laws, its institutions, even the most fundamental guarantee of voting was unavailable to us. Today there are still people who don't like us and some bad people in government, but for the most part those days are gone. It is our own individual and cultural weaknesses that prohibit our progress.

"We kill ourselves with gang violence and AIDS; we choose to drop out of high school at a rate as high as 70% in some areas; and we choose to project an image of our mothers and daughters as sex-obsessed whores to the world for 30 pieces of silver."

Walt realizes that he was talking about rap videos and Walt's profiting from representing Rappers. The point was that his hands were not clean. Even though that was true, it made him even angrier.

"OK, Reverend, let's do this. Your new friends, your conservative buddies, are the same preachers that blessed the congregation on Sunday after the lynching and picnic on Saturday. Their demonic morality saw no contradiction between the beating and killings of Blacks and being a good Christian. This lineage goes all the way back to slavery before the Civil War, a time of rape, child-murders, enslavement, and stealing the labor of a whole life and its dreams. We lived through the hate, fear and ignorance of Jim Crow laws.
"

"In the same way they justified all the atrocities committed against us without it disturbing their values or their faith. They wear blinders, as now the poor, middle-class children and the elderly suffer and die with your blessing. There is no moral compass, only complicity with the worst instincts in man, and the prince on lies."

This debate was the last thing Norman wanted. As one of the President's advisors, he has spoken at colleges all over the country and abroad, written three successful books on Social Darwinism, failures of the global information age and of course "What I Can Do for My Country." So he hates feeling compelled to engage these clowns. He knows it's a losing proposition. Freud could not psychoanalyze his relatives, Jesus could not preach in Nazareth, and he will not win this argument for the same reason. In the town you grew up, you're just another guy. He can feel everyone waiting for him to respond. He tries to cut it off. "Reverend, let me walk you to your car."

Slim said, "Norm, I thought the Reverend was already saved. You aint got to save him."

"Slim I'm not …."

The phone rang. It's a special ring; it's the President. Norman walked away in mid-sentence, listened, jumped into his car and left. The President had a special assignment for him, something about a Clone.

Chapter Four

I awaken somewhere between a hangover and a dream. I see silhouettes in cloudy shadows of light, drifting in jerky waves of motion. My head pounds and my eyelids quiver, resisting my efforts to pry them open. They open slightly and then fall heavily. I try again.

"Hello, Clint," I hear in the darkness of my mind. "I see you have decided to join us. We have missed you."

That voice sends a chill through my body, and the pounding in my head intensifies. It is him, my Keeper, my Master. "Call me Father", he said to me before making me a human lab rat. I try to stand and then to move my arms but I can barely feel my arms or my legs. I would not be certain that I moved at all except I now feel exhausted. I can do nothing but sleep.

In my dream I am in another part of the universe. I see stars and planets, streaking comets and gases of different shades and colors. Suddenly, irrationally, a cloud appears and on it are castles and playgrounds. I can hear the voices of happy children. I hear harps and see heaven. Soaring out of the clouds are two angels, blond and cherubic, lovingly cradling two children, the children I lived with. I reach out to touch them and my hand hits glass. They laugh as they pass me. I see that I am an embryo in a jar and I am floating on top of a slimy clear liquid. The liquid gets higher and higher in the jar; I am going to drown. Suddenly my jar starts to move incredibly fast towards earth, like a space capsule. As I plummet through the earth's atmosphere the jar gets hotter. The liquid in my jar is now part steam, and the rest is boiling. I cry out; my scream is high pitched and eerie. The glass hits a tree and shatters; I land in a field, wiggling around like a fish on a hook.

When I awake the second time, I am lying down. There is a tube in my arm and I can hear voices in the distance. I decide to keep my eyes closed and to listen. All I can hear is mumbling as the voices fade off into the distance. I open my eyes and look around the room. The lights are off. In the dark I reflect upon my life.

I was never part of a family; I was part of a plan. At age three I was brought to the home of Lt. Colonel Baker. Mrs. Baker had given birth to twins two years before and therefore had to endure the terrible twos, times two. She was a hollow, cold woman who could not feel love; the most she could muster was duty.

She was devoted to the routines of the twins' lives. She bought the most nutritious foods, read books on infant care, spent time reading to them and holding them. She mimicked all the actions of a loving mother, hoping one day the feelings would come.

As a partner in marriage she brought the same diligence. She was the perfect hostess, advocate and manager. She guided the Colonel through the maze of intangibles that were often more important to a successful career than the job itself. She worked out four times a week, ate nutritious foods and rarely said no to sex. She was a good military wife. Duty had become her life. She could not remember a fantasy; she could not envision happiness.

She kept an immaculate home. She had a maid and a gardener, whom she replaced frequently. While in her employ, however, she treated them firmly yet cordially, always aware of her image. These domestics talk to each other.

Yet in the quiet scream that was her life, there was one outlet to her pain, a place where she could lose control, scream, belittle, torture and demean. I was that outlet. I watched with amazement as she humbly accepted compliments for adopting a child while having those twins to raise.

"Oh, you must be some kind of saint," a neighbor said.

"I know he is a very distant relative, but when I saw his helpless handsome face, I just fell in love with him right there," she lied as she put her arm around me.

I winced from her hug, partly from the hypocrisy and partly from the bruise on my left shoulder acquired the previous night when I was lovingly thrown against the dresser.

The twins, Junior and Ruth, mimicked their mother's disdain for me and worked together to make my life miserable. If they broke something or took something forbidden, one would invariably say they saw me do it and the other would say, "Me too."

Those two words "Me too," repeated again and again, were always the prelude to more punishment and victimization. "Me too" crystallized my isolation and became a bazaar mantra for the loneliness and injustice in my life.

From birth until joining the Bakers at age three, I nearly died eight times. The first two times were attributed to my Cloning. Although death occurs rarely now from this process there is still danger. The other six times were the result of the follies of the Domestic Uberman Mission, the name given to the multi-billion dollar secret project that created me.

They first created a profile of what the ideal male weapon should be: loyal, athletic, analytical, resilient, selfless, handsome, agile, merciless and cunning. After years of refining the selection process, they chose three men as potential 'sires'. They then researched their family histories and followed and gathered information about them for years before deciding on Marcellus Armstrong as the baseline specimen for creating my Prototype.

They were certain they had made the right selection when he showed up at the Project site demanding to know what was going on. Here was a guy smart enough to figure out that he was being followed and astute enough to uncover his pursuers. He had begun following their field agents and tapping their communication. He researched names and found out what each person's former Projects and research areas were. He followed cars, created phony ID cards and was now the hunter.

He was only the baseline of what I was to become. My DNA was altered to make my lung capacity larger, my reflexes sharper, my muscles bigger, my resistance to disease stronger, my healing powers more rapid, and to reduce my need for sleep. I received DNA from other humans, plants and animals and my body went through intense rejections almost killing me several times. I was even given DNA designed to increase my body's ability to thwart rejection. Twice when I faced death, my heart stopped, I saw no tunnel, no bright light, I felt no warmth or intense love, and no relatives waiting to greet me. I felt pain and I felt alone, as I have all my life, as I do now.

I have always wanted to get away. Not the escaping and eluding that I did to avoid capture. I mean I actually lust to see places new and different. I have traveled to Egypt and Peru, Greece and Jamaica, Zambia, Equator and observed the squalor and pageantry of nature. I observed hungry animals devouring frightened ones, with no animosity or vendetta, no noble cause or patriotic duty.

Kills consist of jaws clamping, the loud snap of breaking bone, claws ripping flesh, followed by the release of heat from the inner body into the air as vapor, blood oozing crimson red on the grass and soaking the soil, and life departing the eyes. The killer leaves meat where there once was a living being.

I lived in Zambia for a year hoping to derive meaning from these brutal exchanges. I thought that my powerful, genetically engineered eyes might see a soul departing or serenity come to the prey. I wondered if I would ever have the detachment of the lion. I wondered whether I would be reincarnated as an antelope or face eternal damnation.

"Clint, my boy, I see that you are finally with us." It is the Colonel, now General Baker.

"Being with you has never been good," I say.

"Yes, Clint, but it has always been necessary and it is necessary today. You have not done too bad for yourself dating a Senator's daughter. I am not too fond of mongrels, but she has a primitive appeal."

"Thank you, and how is that gay son of yours? Any grandchildren yet? And Ruth, was that her third abortion?" I smile and glare at him, as his eyes blink rapidly, the only sign of the hurt and anger my words have caused.

I remember how Junior would fondle the maids and the cooks in vain attempts to feel surges of manhood. A maid and the cook's daughter were beaten in attempted rapes that turned into vicious assaults when he could not become erect. He found that he liked instilling fear, so he began to skip the foreplay and began beating maids and weaker children in school. It was while wrestling on the floor, trying to overcome a smaller boy, that he achieved his first erection.

This made him like fighting even more. He loved military life as it gave honor to his violent instincts and an ample supply of discreet, well-built men.

Ruth was raised to believe that every sexual urge was forbidden and unclean. So she detested herself and felt ashamed with each honest emotion. She began to drink as the only way to become uninhibited. While drunk she flirted with boys without shame. The next morning submerged in guilt but still pure she would refuse to return their calls. This made her life just as frustrating.

Then she started going to parties on the other side of town. There she found men who didn't take no for an answer or who would ply her with drinks until she was nearly unconscious. She could then rationalize that she was not responsible for the pleasure she received. She was drunk or overpowered. This self-imposed victimization worked for a while. Her father had one guy arrested, another beaten. But eventually she and the whole family had to accept that she liked booze and dick. This was especially hard on her mother who abhorred her shameless behavior but envied her passion and freedom. She began to hate her daughter. It is the only real passion she would feel until her death.

"Do you want to know where your girlfriend is or do you want more time to insult your family?" General Baker asks.

"It appears that you want me to know, so why don't you just tell me?"

"She is with her father. Two FBI Agents brought her home. He was told that she was abducted for ransom but rescued as a result of brilliant law enforcement. It appears we had been watching these guys for some time.

They are terrorists, he was told, who have nothing against his daughter. They just hate freedom.

So if you don't cooperate, Clint, we will simply kidnap her again and tell him that the terrorist want to exchange her for other terrorist who are in jail.."

I am relieved that she is safe. "What do you want from me?" I ask.

"We need an L.G.."

An L.G. is a lone gunman needed to assassinate a high profile target. The assassin must have a blank slate. Operatives then use documentation to construct an identity for the shooter that is consistent with the murder.

It will be the 10th kill for me. My first kill I felt like a young boy catching his first fish. I felt nothing for the worm on the hook or the gasping fish, only the delight of having caught one. I could not wait to tell Father, "I caught one, I caught one!"

The next kill I wanted to be perfect. I imagined that the world's best detectives would attempt to solve the case and I wanted to leave no clues. There were no fibers, no blood, nothing traceable--just a pin prick of a rare poison as I jostled through the crowd at Grand Central Station. With three through five, I created obstacles that didn't exist and gave my victims advantages they were unaware of, so the kill would be more exciting and challenging. Six and seven were just a day at the office.

Then on kill number eight I began to change. The change did not come as some sudden revelation. I did not have an epiphany or near death experience. It was more like when you reach puberty and first discover that you like girls. Its like a switch is turned on and you no longer look at women or the world in the same way again.

Joel Mainstreet was the first kill I saw as a life. He was a Vice-President of an oil company who was about to spill the beans to a Senate Investigating Committee.

I studied his background as I do with all my targets. As I reviewed the data I began to see a wonderful life, a great family, dedication to his work and community, a guy who was a giver and had life figured out. I did something I had never done before; I actually got to know him personally since he was easy to know. I befriended him, I idealized his life, holding it up as the model of what mine should but would never be. Then I allowed the seed of envy to grow in me so that I could do my job. I made myself hate him and then I killed him; I staged his death as a suicide.

I went to his burial. There were so many people there that I could easily blend into the crowd. Many reluctant tears were shed, some sobbing openly. Heads were bowed in respect, admiration and love.

The damage I had done was clear and painful. I wondered what kind of a person I was who could cause such harm. I wondered what I was. This was my state of mind when I made my final kill. I made errors that almost led to my capture. After I killed him I felt dead inside.

So I began to run. I tried to outrun the pain that was in my heart and the pursuers that were at my heels. It appears I will never escape either. My bloody dreams always begin with red paint and end with convulsions and sweat. My captors are relentless and powerful. I may never escape my Karma or my shame. I live certain that no one, except maybe Sara, will cry tears for me.

"Clint, what's the matter with you? Did you hear what I said?"

"Uh, yes, Colonel . . ., or I guess I should say General now, right? I was just a little groggy from whatever you gave me to knock me out." I feel wide awake now.

"We didn't just knock you out; we gave you a few tests and a formula to make you a little more honest than you usually are."

"Does this mean I won't be getting a Christmas card?"

"We didn't waste time asking how you felt about me. We asked about where you hide when you try to escape from us and about your reluctance to do what we spent millions training you do to. You are a weapon, plain and simple, no matter how many philosophers and gurus you talk to who tell you different. You were created for one purpose, bred like a Pit Bull or a racehorse. You have a purpose: a duty to serve your country, to defend liberty, to...."

"I do serve my country, but my country is a country of academics creating challenging concepts no matter where they lead us, of people enjoying their right of privacy, choosing their own sexuality, praying or not praying as they see fit and protesting government when they are wrong.

"Your America is intolerant. Its religious leaders hate diversity, free thinking and science. Soldiers, brave and patriotic, some of our finest, die without armor, while those who convinced them that their wars are just, eat fine pastries and live in palaces."

With tightened jaw and fixed eyes, General responds, "You will defend the America that we are now and you will obey orders that are given to you through your chain of command. A soldier cannot disobey orders based on his individual perceptions; that is anarchy. As to your attack on commerce: America is the richest country in the world and apparently we have allowed enough freedom of academia and technology so that you could be created. Now here's what will happen. If you don't help us, we will kill your girlfriend in a most unpleasant manner; we will send her to a couple of Columbian enforcers who really know what torture is. If you help us, this will be your last job."

"How do I know we will be safe if I do this?"

"She has already been released. We know her routines, people and places, you know, the standard stuff. We can pick her up anytime we wish. As for you, I will give you original documents, sufficient to expose our entire operation. If I don't keep my word, you can go public."

I take the documents. I know what the General's offer really means. Either I have been assigned a suicide mission or they intend to kill me right after I complete the assassination. They will never allow me to be in a position to blackmail them. The documents are fakes.

I am not afraid to die. In fact, a violent death seems fair. I have taken many lives and participated in an organization designed to take lives for the greater good. Yet I now face a paradox in which I will have to take a life to save a life. I now face this choice, the choice that every soldier faces, asking myself whether it is ok to kill for love.

Killing for love is the best reason to kill, whether for love of country or for the special people you protect by your sacrifice. Duty seems less substantial. Should one kill because they are obligated to? Killing in anger, bloodlust or hate has no virtue, certainly no nobility. Yes, love is certainly the best reason to kill and if you are not certain you have a soul, love is all there is.

Yet there is an emptiness in dying without wisdom. If I die now I will perish without knowing whether God exists or whether good and evil are forces that can be measured like gravity and light. When I close my eyes, will I awaken as a knowing spirit connected to the creator, or after the pain of death will I cease to exist? For my crimes and my sins, will I suffer torment endlessly through all time, or will I return to earth as an infant, again blind to my destiny, deserving of my plight?

I love the sensations that this life has provided: the touch of a woman, a dive off a cliff, a cool tropical wave, chocolate, sunsets, curiosity, old scotch and hearty laughs. But having experienced all these things it is the great ideas, the vastness of the ocean, the secrets of quantum physics, the mystery of space, life's meaning, God's wisdom, that hold my interest. For all my disconnected pleasures I do not know who I am or why I'm here and that is why it would be a shame to die.

Chapter Five

Norman Sewell, upon his return to Washington, was immediately met and escorted to the Oval Office. He was concerned about the urgency and secrecy of the President's message.

Although he was also glad to be back. It was sometimes difficult to work with his friend, the President. He knew that he would not have been his first choice for an economic advisor but the President's party insisted on diversity of opinion in the executive branch. Since Norman was a long time friend he was the safest choice. Norm became more of an advisor to the President than an economic strategist. Their views on economic matters couldn't be more different. Norman remembered the President saying, "I want someone who can present another point of view but, more importantly, I want someone who I can trust." Their economic policy was a practical hybrid that stimulated the economy with labor intensive-jobs and firm restrictions on companies that did not hire American workers.

The President greeted him, smiling faintly, his expression somber. His first nine months in office had been hard on him. He had more lines in his face, his hair was grayer and he had lost weight. Political pundits had characterized this time as the worst time to be President. One reporter actually asked him, "Who would want this job?" Norman felt the same way.

The President asked Norman about his visit home and Norm highlighted the good and left out the bad. After a few more minutes of small-talk the President said, "Norm, the United States is involved in three wars started by your party during the last three terms. The first war, we were scared and conned into supporting. The people wanted proof. They said 'You don't want the smoking gun to be a mushroom cloud.' We went to war and then Iraq elected a government that was economically and politically tied to Iran. Iran had nuclear ambitions and was proceeding with its plans. The U.S., seeking to destroy Iran's nuclear capability, bombed the wrong site, killing about 300 people.

"Iran stated that since it had no capacity to respond to the United States on American soil, it would attack troops still stationed in Iraq.

Iraq's leaders shouted some rhetoric about not compromising the integrity of its borders but did little to stop large-scale Iranian incursions into its territory.

"Frankly, it could have done little to stop Iran's forces, even if it wanted to. America sent more soldiers. Our European allies refused to send troops. America asked Turkey for support and it refused. So it asked Israel. They were extremely reluctant but the former President promised that this war would end terrorism in their borders forever.

"So began the third front of the war with sporadic clashes with Muslims in France, Germany and Russia. You know the history."

Of course, Sewell thought. *I wonder why the President is sharing this. It's like he needs to talk his way into the problem. Yeah, he's pacing, not making much eye contact. Whatever it is he has to say, it must be bad.* "Yes sir," Norman said.

The President continued, "Despite years of war we were ill-prepared for the expanded challenge. Years of defense spending as giveaways to defense contractors had produced $700 billion dollar Defense Department spending on obsolete weaponry and star wars defense systems that didn't work. Supplemental appropriations of $100-200 billion helped favored companies get contracts but left soldiers unprotected.

"Cronyism meant that at the CIA, the UN, the State Dept, World Bank and Diplomatic Corps we had the worst person for the job, making our non-military response inept."

Norm did not want to interrupt but wanted answers. "Sir?"

The President held up his hand and said, "Let me do this my way, Norm." He continued.

"The people's rights have diminished as quickly as their wealth. Anyone who was alleged to have criticized our government was thrown in jail. It got worse after the incident."

"You mean the Right Tag fire?" Norman asked.

"Yeah, when that discount store in downtown D.C. was blown up, everyone went crazy. The Right Tag fire received 24-hour media coverage, with hawks saying, 'I told you we needed to strengthen the laws to make us safe and media needs to stop questioning us. We are at war.' It turned out to be some nut who was mad at the owner but the public didn't learn that for years.

"In the meantime, my party cowered. 90% of us agreed to anything the former administration proposed. We sold out the American people.

"We now have a majority in Congress. Americans had become so angry with this government that they wanted sweeping changes and bold ideas. Progressives like me were persuaded that we didn't have enough votes to win. So we made a deal with the Democratic Innocuous Council (DIC's). I had to run a middle of the road campaign, not wanting to offend any of the independent voters or strays from the other party that might vote for us.

"So I won while speaking of reconciliation and talks of one big tent. The opposition, however, was now even more vicious and was as committed as the minority party. As the opposition party in Congress they challenge the constitutionally of almost any law, hoping for a reversal by the Supreme Court, which they control.

"They engaged in personal attacks and were eagerly and openly disloyal to me, the Commander–in-Chief. They make my life hell and don't care that it impedes my ability to save the country that they have all but ruined. Norm, I was prepared for that--not the ferocity and inhumanity of it, because I knew that was coming--but not this." He bowed and shook his head.

Norm was beginning to worry. He had known this man since freshman year at Harvard. He had always been great in a crisis, so his anxiety made Norm a little anxious too. He tried to relax. The President's intercom flashed.

He said, "I'll be just a moment," and stepped outside the door.

Norm had to wait for an hour, feeling frustrated about being kept in the dark. But as time passed he turned his attention to the office itself. He was still awed at the power of the Oval Office and thought of the many great men who had sat in that chair.

The President returned and said, "Sorry, Norm." He was accompanied by the Director of the Secret Service. He sat down. Norman thought this was unusual since when agents were in the room, they were always standing and the Director was never in the room.

The only reason Norman recognized him is because he had met him at the Inauguration. Norman shook his hand and introduced himself.

"Hi, Norman, Daniel Bloom here. We met at the Inauguration."

The President said suddenly, "I'm going to leave you two to talk." Norman turned in his chair and started to speak but the President said, "Relax, Norm. Daniel will explain everything."

Norman looked at Daniel who said, "Follow me."

Norm and Daniel exited through another door to an area of the White House Norm had never seen. It led to a secluded, oddly lit room. The walls were gray and made of metal. There was more peeling than paint as if someone painted them decades ago. Norm felt as if he were inside a vault. The room was bare except for a desk, some folding chairs and a bookshelf, which he thought was odd since no one would come here to read. Daniel began speaking.

"Norman, the President has extreme confidence in you. He finds you intelligent, loyal and dependable. But that would not be enough to place you in the position of confidence you are to be entrusted with today. We need to also call on your patriotism, honor and commitment to justice."

Norm waited and held eye contact.

"As you know, there have always been forces that thought that power should be kept in as few hands as possible. It began with the Constitutional Convention and those who wanted to restrict voting only to those who had land. Then after Shays' Rebellion and all the other skirmishes around the colonies, the new U.S. government was forced by the people to include a Bill of Rights. We went on to the Civil War, the assassination of Lincoln, Woman's Suffrage, the labor movement, the inclusion of immigrants, and Civil Rights. Each step along the way opposed vigorously by two types of people: those who felt that they lost something by expanding opportunity to others and secondly the corporate class that knew that the expansion of freedom and education meant higher wages, fringe benefits, more unions and more demands from workers, driving down profits.

"This second group is determined to keep power at all cost and have lost faith in your party's ability to maintain power for them. They have chosen to intervene by assassinating the President."

Norman momentarily stood rigid. His heart started racing, his muscles suddenly tensed, his breathing became shallow, and his mouth felt bone dry. He stared blankly as he backed up slowly until his heel hit the chair. With his eyes fixed on Daniel, he grasped the arms of the chair and lowered himself into the seat. "Go ahead," he muttered.

"The people I spoke to you about earlier were responsible for the American Eugenics movement. They have always been keen on creating a master race and isolating the best genes. So when Human Cloning became a serious possibility, they funded much of the initial research, in and out of the country."

"What does this have to do with killing the President?" Norm asked.

Daniel could feel Norm's anxiety. "I'm getting there, Norman, but first it's important that you know what we're up against."

"These Eugenics guys continued their work in the dark. They used the third world as their lab. The mice in the experiments were young girls that no one would miss. They were given research grants through the CIA, National Academy of Sciences and the Department of Defense. Defense began to get more and more of these contracts since their books were such a mess no one knew where to find anything. Politicians on both sides wanted to look strong on defense for so long that no one dared question where the money was going.

"Well, decades ago, the Defense Department started a Cloning program called Ultimate Soldier. The idea was to breed weapons. They used the genetic material of many men in different combinations hoping to create an assassin-a soldier who would have super-human ability and intelligence."

"How did they fare?" Norman asked.

"There were many missteps and incarnations of the program, but eventually they were successful. The Domestic Uberman Mission is its name now and they have been responsible for some very impressive work. One persistent problem, however, is that their creations, although initially amazing, become erratic, psychotic or suicidal. They have a shelf-life shorter than an NFL player and cost a lot to make."

"So is one of these things, one of these Ubermen, after the President?" Norman asked.

"Yes," Daniel replied. "And from what I hear, he's one of the best."

Norman listened intently as Daniel told him all that they knew about the plot to assassinate the President. He heard every detail but his mind was in a fog. It's like the words were being typed on a cloud.

As he drove home he thought about his involvement in an incident that could change the course of world history and he thought, "Why me?"

Chapter Six

Daniel Bloom had been working 16-hour days following leads, collecting data, thinking and re-thinking all possible scenarios. *There will be no assassination on my watch,* he resolved to himself.

But trying to identify the potential assassin was complicated. He was investigating a project that was not supposed to exist so there were few people likely to know anything; those who knew anything were least likely to talk.

Mostly he did not know whom he could trust. The opposition had many people in high places, reflecting their years in power. In addition, they had moles within the agencies that spied on their colleagues, making sure that the federal agencies maintained their view of patriotism. Since he was not sure when the attempt would occur, it made heightened security necessary at every public appearance.

He had one very important thing in his favor, however; the opposition thought that he was one of them. Only a select few of his friends knew his true feelings and values and he was on his way to see two of them now. They were his mirror and his window. They would spend a weekend at the lake, taking a pause from the velocity of his life to gain energy and insight, have some laughs and drink beer.

J.D. and Mike are his closest friends. Mike was Irish-Catholic, born on the lower East Side in New York. Most of his relatives were small-time crooks or big-time cops. When he was young, he didn't know which he wanted to be. He was always a big guy; he had lifted weighs and played a little college football. He could have gone pro if he were faster. After getting into trouble for a couple of misdemeanor assaults after barely completing college, he found he had too much of a conscience to be a crook, so he joined the force.

With both a college degree and nepotism on his side, Mike rose through the ranks quickly. He could have probably been the Police Commissioner one day, despite the fact that he never put much energy or thought into his job.

That all changed on his 28th birthday, the day Reagan was shot. He had always admired the man. Reagan came out of that Hollywood wasteland to speak for real Americans. He wished he could have been there to protect him. Instead, he watched the city's neighborhoods birth criminals like a putrid womb. He was tired of cleaning up the mess only to step in it a few minutes later. So after his old partner was killed in a routine bust, he began to think about doing something more meaningful. He joined the Secret Service and grew up fast. He was now considered one of their most dedicated and skilled agents. He and Daniel respected each other's work and eventually became good friends.

J.D. and Daniel were childhood friends. Their fathers both worked in the coal mines in West Virginia. Their fathers detested the mine guards and the low wages. They shed tears as mines were shut down with men still trapped inside. They armed themselves to defend themselves against the bosses goons and as children they held their fathers hands and sang union songs. They were part of a tight-knit community where there were few resources. They went to the same schools, played the same sports and on occasion courted the same girl. But after high school Daniel went to college and met and married Cordelia, whose family owned a big farm in Pennsylvania. Her father was sick and was in danger of losing the farm. Daniel put his plans on hold, moved to Pennsylvania and eventually managed the farm. His friend JD loved farming; it reminded him of the many times he spent on his grandfather's farm in Mississippi. When Daniel was trying to revive his wife's farm, JD helped out a lot.

It was backbreaking and demanding work. JD seemed made for it though. When the farm started to thrive, JD left for Mississippi to build his grandfathers farm. He was successful making deals for land that no one thought was profitable. He tended and nurtured that nearly barren earth year after year until it produced.

So when the city government decided to use Eminent Domain to seize his land and give it to some Agribusiness he fought back hard. He organized other farmers and ran against the Mayor and won.

Serving as Mayor was a part-time job but one JD took seriously. He found he was good at organizing and he was good with people. He thought about how hard his fellow farmers and coal miners worked and how the fat cats were always making deals to give what little they had away. He knew that politicians were using gimmicks like deregulation to make their jobs less safe. He knew that paying a $2000 deductible before you could use your medical benefits meant that more people would go to work sick. And he realized that corporations weren't patriotic; they would create jobs where it was cheapest—usually abroad--while we waved American flags made in China. Our sons went off to fight the wars; their sons stayed home and closed our farms. JD rose in power to become Lt. Governor of Mississippi.

Daniel met with JD and Mike at a cabin so lavish it could hardly be called a cabin.

J.D. brought a bottle of Jack in one hand and a duffle bag in the other, looked around and said, "Ooh-ee, Dannie boy, you done went and got you a double-wide. Hey Mike, how you?"

Daniel got up and hugged him. Mike tried to shake his hand but J.D. hugged him too.

"Danny boy, I hope we gonna do some huntin while we're here," JD said as he threw his duffle bag and coat in the closet.

Daniel said, "I don't know, we got this city boy here. One of us might end up getting shot."

Mike smiled. "If you guys having possum for dinner, I can go get me some McDonalds. I can get you guys a Mc-raccoon or something."

Daniel said, "At least we can agree on the Jack. Let me get you guys some glasses."

Mike said, "Congratulations on the election, JD. I heard that all 20 people voted for you."

JD poured another drink. "I don't know if we got all 20; I owed two of them ole boys some money."

They laughed and JD continued, "Yer right though. Your murder rate is bigger than most towns in Mississippi. We're small but we ain't got your big city problems."

"We can't live in the woods all the time, J.D.; not me anyway," Mike said.

"It's not about where, it's about how we live," J.D. responded. "We not only speak to our neighbors, we go to church with them, we went to school with them and my grand-pappy knew their grandparents. We know who's who and what's what."

Mike said, "Hey, if you're real Irish, somebody knows somebody who knows ya. But in a big city, if you got Niggers, Chinks, Ricans, Jews, and Homo's living like you do it would be just like me living with just Irish, huh?"

"Yeah, I guess, except for Blacks. Time was we knew who their families were too; we just didn't mix."

"Yeah, you knew them caused you owned them."

Mike laughed.

J.D. responded more seriously, "You know, Mike, not many of us owned slaves but many of them slaves ate better than we did. We were free but that sometimes meant free to starve. Lots of times we ended up sharecropping at that same plantation. Working side by side with slaves makes it hard to feel good about what you've done with your life. So when you're that poor and that hurt you need something to feel better than, so we kept the Blacks in check."

Mike said, "Personally I don't care what you did to those bastards. They live like roaches; they steal crumbs and live in garbage."

"Mike, I'm not the NAACP but I will say this: They went through a lot of shit, some of them with their heads held high. But so have most southerners. The average White man in the South is not making nearly what Irish, Jews and Italians are earning in this country and we don't get no help from the federal government like Blacks. We are still struggling and for a long time we had no one we could depend on but ourselves."

Daniel joined the conversation. "Who can you depend on now"?

J.D. said, "Anyone smart enough to realize that the government and these corporations are handing us a load of shit. They are giving more money to rich folk than they ever gave to Blacks. Look, I'm getting riled up. Can we talk about something else?"

Daniel goaded him. "What about the wars? How do you feel about them, J.D."?

J.D. knows Daniel is messing with him but he can't stop himself from taking the bait. "Those damn bastards. They killing the best boys this country got. Sending 363 tons of cash on pallets and don't even get a receipt, yet they ain't got nothing but excuses when it comes to protecting our boys.

"Mike, do you know how many funerals I had to bow my head at for guys dying who didn't need to be dead. You were a cop. Suppose your buddies was dying cause there were no bulletproof vests but every year that budget just got fatter and fatter?"

"Mike shook his head. "I support the troops!"

"Yeah, Mike, so do I. We just need the government to do that too."

Daniel looked at the time and said, "Normally I like hearing you guys shoot the shit but I've got something here I can't get wrong."

Mike said, "Sure, boss, whatever you need. Let me just drain the weasel."

As Mike went to the bathroom, JD asked, "What's up, buddy?"

Daniel replied, "Remember when we were kids up in that tree trying to catch a glimpse of Barbara Jean's tits?"

"Yeah."

"Well, I'm going to need you to have your eyes even more wide open and not fall out the tree."

When Mike returned Daniel explained in great detail the threat facing the nation. They knew they had to find the assassin and find him fast.

II

Less than fifty miles away from Bloom and his friends, Clint is in training and proclaims to himself: I am in the best condition of my life. I have just run twelve miles and it feels like walking. I begin to increase my speed. My senses are sharp; I hear small animals in the woods at the same time that I listen to my heartbeat. I throw a few punches in the air. I run backwards for half a mile and then turn around. I sprint for a hundred yards and I am breathing normally 10 seconds later. I stop, walk a little, stretch and head back. I dart through the woods moving stealthily from tree to tree. I roll, I attack. I sit silently for thirty minutes absorbing the rhythms of the forest.

I return to the compound. I am scheduled for more tactical and weapons training. It is ludicrous. There are only three men alive who have more high-level kills than I do. They mentored and molded me decades ago. The only joy in this charade is that it reminds me how good I am at this, how perfect I am for what I do. I am a warrior.

My genes and my training, nature and nurture, compel me. I pulse with energy, I yearn for action. What is it then that resists?

Certainly it is not a conscience. There was no love in my childhood, no ethics. Sure I read philosophy and the great novels as a man, but one does not arrive at moral convictions purely through intellect. The intellect would simply make a rationalization for my sins. No, this is something stronger, more real but less finite. Could it be my soul?

I am both elated at the possibility and confused at the irony of discovering God as I am training for murder. I try to let the elation linger but I have no time. I shower, dress and hurry to the makeshift conference room. There are five men in the room. No names are given. The project is named Tsunami. My codename is Butterfly. They talk more about me than to me.

"Wednesday is the target date. There are several high profile events on Tuesday so security will be lax. We know the vehicle and the route and have the itinerary. Any changes in plan will be sent to us by our man inside. The activity is at a university. It is an outdoor venue with two primary and four secondary areas of opportunity."

A second man says, "I have reviewed the previous flights of the Butterfly and this is consistent with his patterns and abilities. In fact, he is ideally suited to this assignment."

I listen to their logistics, research and assumptions. On paper they have planned everything to the smallest detail; on paper any one of them could do my job. But it is never easy. There are dozens of traps, coincidences and oddities that could terminate the mission and end my life. It is only my instincts and experience that can prevent me from being caught. It is my will and my lust for success that have made me their best assassin.

I am not sure of the date, but the target is clear. They want me to assassinate the President. I am sure that I will do everything in my power to keep him alive and to destroy the evil that produced me. For the first time ever, I will pray.

Chapter 7

At the Senator's apartment in D.C. Sara pleaded, "Dad, have you heard anything yet?"

He ached from seeing the sadness in her eyes. "No nothing yet" He wished he could help her but all he could do was console her.

"Have you heard anything from the FBI?"

"I talked with Henderson; he is a real good man. As soon as we have something of substance, believe me, sweetheart, I'll let you know."

He was lying. Initially when Sara wanted to go to the police, he stopped her. He said he would handle it. He was afraid of scandal, the scandal of the press finding out who Sara was. More importantly, no one seemed to know who Clint was. He could be Mafia or a Terrorist who was manipulating his daughter to get to him, he thought.

Clint was an unknown who could ruin him. So he hired some of the private security, black ops guys who would be discreet and would not blackmail him. Unfortunately, very little information was coming in and Sara seemed more desperate for answers each day.

"What about the black Hummers? Any leads on them?"

"No, nothing."

Although Sara was distraught and she trusted her father, she had strong intuitive signals that her father was lying. "Can I go with you the next time you meet with Henderson?"

"No, Sara, I want to keep you out of this. I can handle this without these guys asking you all kinds of personal and embarrassing questions."

"I am never embarrassed and even if I could be, embarrassment would be the least of my concerns now. Are you concerned about what the press might do to you?"

"Yes, Sara, because of what I do I must always be concerned about that but my main concern is for you."

"And Clint," she reminded him.

"And Clint," he echoed.

She looked into his eyes, and knew he was definitely hiding something, but so was she. She had not told him who Clint was. She would never betray him, not even to save him. "Dad, I'm going back to the hotel." She kissed him on the cheek. "Please call me the minute you hear anything."

Sara was ashamed of herself. She knew that she was not behaving like an evolved spiritual being. She had acted more like a teen in a horror movie. She was an emotional wreck.

She knew that she needed to reclaim herself. She knew she needed to pray and meditate in order to focus her energy on the problem at hand. She remembered well the lessons she had taught others: "You don't change anything without until you change from within." Her emotional and chaotic state of mind would only create more instability, not help Clint. Concentration, prayer and meditation would make her efforts productive; seeming coincidences would bring her closer to Clint. The Universe rarely fails the directed will of the caring heart.

She spent a full day in gratitude, giving thanks for her blessings, reaffirming her unconditional faith in God's will and thanking God for delivering Clint to her safe and unharmed. She visualized their meeting again and their embrace. She would do this until her prayers were answered.

Her father took a more traditional approach and it was beginning to get results.

"Senator, we have some information on that missing persons case you were interested in. Where and when can we meet?"

"As soon as possible but not in my office," Townsend said. I have a place on the Maryland shore; let's meet there at 3pm. Does that give you enough time?"

"Sounds fine, Senator," the man replied.

Senator Townsend arrived at 2pm at his family's summer home in Maryland. It was pure decadence and grand simplicity. The white sand had been shipped from Negril. The rocks along the shoreline had been selected, arranged, transported by an architect from the University of Hawaii. Coconut and palm trees were genetically engineered to take the cold of the sometimes harsh Maryland winter.

The effect was overwhelming yet soothing, the envy of any tropical island. It was a place to forget almost anything or to feel connected to everything. It had been too long since he'd let its spell wash over him;

he promised himself he would make plans to spend some time here. He really hoped this thing could be wrapped up today. He needed some time away. The doorbell rang.

"Hello, Senator, this is a beautiful place you have here. I didn't know you could get to a place like this without a plane ticket."

Townsend smiled. "Yeah, it's a great place to relax. Have a seat. Can I get you and your associate anything to drink?"

He looked at the tall, disheveled man who was staring out at the water but had not spoken a word.

His contact said, "Scotch for me. I don't think Jake is drinking. This is the guy I wanted you to meet. Jake, take a seat."

Jake ignored his request and the small talk that followed. He sat cross-legged in front of the huge glass double doors, staring out at the Bay.

"Jake, come on, the Senator doesn't have all day."

Jake shot back a sharp look and then unfolded his lanky body without much effort. He sat down, looked briefly at Townsend and then gave his attention to Blackops.

"Senator, I'm happy to report that we have made some progress," Blackops said. "It looked kind of bleak there for a while. We tried police, Interpol, FBI and our own data bases and came up empty. We tried our contacts and put his picture everywhere we could without saying why we were looking, you know what I mean?"

"Yeah, go on," Townsend urged.

He could sense the Senator's impatience. "We got our break yesterday. Jake here says he recognized the picture, and says he used to work with Clint. I think this is big, Senator, but I'll let Jake explain."

Jake mumbled at first and Townsend leaned toward him cupping his ear. Jake spoke up and appeared to be in the middle of a story. "Clint shoulda kept runnin'. I don't know why he came back. They got him. Number 1, but look at him now."

Townsend looked at Blackops and then looked at Jake. Now that he was closer he could see Jake's tiny, hollow eyes, and the subtle rocking and nervous scratching.

Blackops tried to get Jake on point. "Jake, tell him how you know Clint."

"We worked for the government. Yeah, we're federal employees." Jake snickered. "They all thought he was such hot shit, they kissed the ground he walked on."

The Senator and Blackops decided to let him ramble. "He always got the best assignments and the rest of us got dogshit. Remember Tiger Woods, the golfer, and how all people could talk about was his concentration? They would interview the other golfers and ask, 'What do you think about Tiger?'"

"Were you involved in some team sport?" the Senator asked.

"No, I wish we were 'cause then I could have beat him outright. Take speed, for example. You know, I was the fastest of all of us. No, that's why I said golf. You are against other people but not really. You can see your competition but you can't stop him, play defense or distract him. No, your opponent is yourself, your conditioning, your concentration, your mental game and your weaknesses. And him, Clint, he didn't care about nothing. Behind his back we called him ice-block because no matter how much you chipped away you wouldn't find nothing but ice.

"He never mixed with us during group training. Thought he was better than us. He had the answers to questions we never thought of. I guess he was pretty good but they should have given the rest of us a chance."

Jake stopped talking and appeared to be lost in thought. Townsend started to speak but then Jake slammed one hand over the other.

"Look at my hands," he said, momentarily freeing them. Both hands were trembling. "We should get medals and a million dollars each. Police and fireman, they call them heroes. Do they wake up at night running into walls to escape their own terror? Do they smell the odor of flesh burning and bullets whizzing past their ears like mosquitoes? In their heads, do they hear shrill voices saying 'Jake's dead, kill Jake'? Some laugh, some cry, but they all want me dead. I know, I know, you want Clint. Everybody wants Clint." Jake starts he cry.

Townsend thought this guy was insane and was ready to ask Blackops directly for the information, but Jake continued.

"I want a million dollars, man," Jake cried out.

Townsend said, "If you have something valuable, I'll pay you."

"Pay me a million dollars."

"What do you know?"

"Saving the President's life is worth a million, right?"

Townsend looked at Blackops to confirm that this was not just the rambling of Jake's lunatic mind.

Blackops nodded. "Jake was part of a Dept of Defense program that has been a legend for years but no one has ever confirmed it exists. If what Jake says is true, Defense created supermen--correction--super hit men by cloning what they thought was the perfect spy and then adding genetic material from any source that would enhance each spy clone's abilities. These guys supposedly have superhuman strength, speed, healing ability, and muscle recovery time. You know, like in Niche's wet dream."

Townsend was initially stunned but then dozens of questions raced into his head. If Jake was right, Clint was the hit man and the President was the target. "Why is Jake so screwed up?" Townsend asked Blackops.

"I don't know. Apparently, sophisticated cloning can lead to problems like they had with cloning sheep back in the 90s. Something inside goes screwy and they either have mental or physical problems. Or it could be just like Jake said: If you cause enough death and chaos you can go crazy."

"How did this remain a secret for so long?" Townsend asked.

"They kept the secret in two ways: First, they had Generals and full Birds raise these guys as if they were their own kids. They would test and train them at a special location. It was a tight circle and since they were committing murder, everyone involved knew that if they said anything they would be killed.

"Second, even back then it was pretty easy to keep things secret when all you had to say was that there was a war going on and denounce the curious as traitors."

Blackops continued to brief Townsend, who listened in awed disbelief. After the two men left, he sat there thinking and rethinking his next move. Who could he trust? Should he tell the President himself? Would he be safe? Was Sara in love with this murderer? He decided to call Sewell, who was a close friend of the President and someone he knew was not involved with the Defense Department. He would have to feel him out to be sure, but he seemed like the right choice.

The Senator then cancelled his evening appointments and went down to the shore to take a walk on the beach. He watched the sun disappear into the clouds amidst a vivid purple-orange sky. He walked to the house slowly, opened the glass doors and made coffee. He began to drink and he saw that his hands were trembling uncontrollably. After misdialing twice, he reached Sewell.

Norm Sewell's schedule had suddenly become impossible. He had his regular duties as an economic guru at the White House. His mother ,Betty, had suffered a heart attack and he had wanted to be there. Walt was at the hospital every day doing what he could to help his mother and comfort his Dad. Sure they had drifted apart, but Walt was the guy he'd want to be in a foxhole with.

He remembered how Walt used to look out for him when they were kids; this crisis with his mother had drawn them back together. He even considered discussing the assassination plot with him. At that moment his car hit a pothole jarring him and refocusing his thoughts. He pulled up adjacent to the restaurant and spotted the Senator's car. When Townsend first called, he had asked Norman to meet him in front of the Capitol building.

"What's this all about, Senator?" Norman remembered saying.

The Senator walked down the steps toward him and they shook hands. In his palm was a note, which he asked Norman to slip into his pocket. "Norman, read this, and if you don't think I'm crazy meet me tomorrow at two at The Healthy Soul."

The Healthy Soul was a soul food restaurant that had survived gentrification by cooking without transfats and had become chic by offering lattes, wine and light jazz. It was slow at 2pm, however, and they picked a table near enough to the Kenny G–like performer to keep others from overhearing their conversation.

Daniel had thoroughly checked out Townsend and believed he was genuine. He had even discovered that Townsend had a daughter no one knew about. Still, Sewell wanted to be careful. He wanted to get all the info he could without giving any away. He also wanted to determine if Senator Townsend could be trusted enough to become part of the team, since the team was really small.

"Thanks for seeing me, Norman"

"How could I not, Senator? This is as serious as it gets."

Townsend looked around then leaned in and spoke. Townsend told Norman about Jake and Blackops. He told him the main points and then colored between the lines.

After receiving assurance that Jake and Black-ops were authentic Norman said, "I need to get more information from Blackops and then I will meet with him. But there's no doubt in my mind that Jake needs to be contained and interrogated."

"Are you going to tell the President?" Townsend asked. "It seems like the FBI and the Secret Service should be brought in on this."

Norman was thinking about Bloom. He needed to get this information to him. "Senator, I will take care of everything. Please do not mention this to anyone else. I will keep you informed." Sewell began to rise from his chair.

Townsend grabbed his sleeve as he was rising. "There's one more thing. I'm pretty sure the assassin is in love with Sara Kahn and may try to contact her."

Daniel Bloom was listening intently to the conversation from an undisclosed location. He had two active bugs on Sewell, two in his car, a bug in his office, one in his cell phone, five in the house and one in his briefcase. He had determined that Sewell was not a particularly brave man, and this would make him practically useless in a crisis. He had fair planning abilities but was easily deceived. So Bloom wanted all the information Sewell had without any interference. Planting bugs was the perfect way to get it.

When the men finished talking, Bloom picked up the phone. "Sandy, I want you to research a Jake Wobbler and get more info on the Senator's daughter--our eyes only--and I need it yesterday."

He hung up the phone and sat there for a moment. The image of Reagan being shot and the film of the Kennedy assassination emerged from his memory. "Sandy, I'm coming down."

Chapter Eight

Sara sat uneasily in her chair. She shifted her weight from side to side, crossing and re-crossing her legs. Her head turned as each customer entered the store. She loosened her hair and it cascaded down her back. Men looked at her greedily and longingly, and she wondered why. She had done little self-care, devoting herself to finding Clint. She had been praying, meditating and fasting. In her mind's eye, she looked a wreck.

Her Dad had finally called her yesterday. He said he would have a car pick her up. She wondered why he had selected a Clone Bar. The place was decorated with a poor man's vision of elegance. Overstated and overdone, everything cost but nothing fit. The Bar décor screamed conflict in contrast to the quiet temperament of its customers.

Clones became drunk very easily but were docile, an affect of the cloning process. Clones would have mostly been just like any other human except for government intervention. The Food and Drug Administration required that cloned humans be identified just like cloned cattle and sheep. They had patents with corporate logo's underneath their arms. When a few clones became criminal, it was disproportionately reported on the news. Politicians labeled them freakish threats to the society, although the number of Clones committing criminal acts was no more than with any other group of Americans. This led to legislation requiring frontal lobe inserts, which made Clones more obedient, passive and concrete.

Occasionally their inner aggressive instincts would emerge and be blurted out like Tourret's Syndrome. Domestic Clones--the primary patrons of the bar--became more sexual when drunk. Men who could not afford to own Domestics often met them here. The men offered them hope of marriage or an independent life as their paid companions. Clone pimps lurked outside trying to seduce or abduct them, so the women traveled in packs.

Sara felt tense. She decided to relax a little and started breathing deeply. She asked the waiter for water and soup. Two Clone women at the next table were drunk. They were listening intently to the conversation of the couple across from Sara. The women were attractive, middle-aged Donna Cleaver Clones, the second-most preferred of all the models. Every Cleaver Clone was maternal and trained by their corporate manufacturers to be nurturing. She baked fresh bread, did the ironing, redecorated tastefully and—in short-- spoiled her owners rotten. Her melodic voice called you to dinner and she listened compassionately to your smallest problems. Of course, you were free to express your Oedipus fantasy to her ultimate delight and she would make the bed and tuck you in afterwards.

The two Cleavers were eying a fat balding man with a skinny tie. They watched him sit down with another woman after politely asking if he could join her. They giggled when they noticed that one of his shirt buttons had given way revealing the mound of hair on his ample belly. He, like many, was after the #1 domestic female Clone, the Hailey Monroe. His face dripped sweat, although there was plenty of air.

"You are such a beauty. You deserve to have everything the world has to offer. I would really love to see you on your free time."

Her fixed, pretty eyes evaluated him. "Sir, I thank you for your kind words, but I have been exclusively purchased."

"Of course, of course," he said, "but no one will know and I will be more grateful than you can imagine."

The Donna Cleavers whispered, "You know, those Monroe's are just whores. Look at that waste of a man –whore monger. They wouldn't have to change the towels. Monroe and Monger". They giggle and put their hands over their mouths.

"Sara?"

She turned and answered cautiously, "Priest?" She stood and gave him a hug. Continuing to hold on, she let her hands slide down his back to embrace his hands and said, "I was praying to the Universe for an answer. You weren't even in my mind but I am sure God has sent you."

He looked deeply into her eyes. "If I am the answer, what is the question?"

She thought for a moment, remembering that his questions had answers hidden inside them. Her first thought was to respond, *How can I save the man I love and remove the danger that I know is coming?* But instead she responded, "Why do I lack courage and faith in this situation?"

"You know the answer," Priest said, almost in a whisper.

"Yes," said Sara. "I should care equally for all God's creations and I am guilty for caring so much about this one man. When I am feeling guilty and selfish, I will attract only guilty and selfish energy." She paused, then asked, "What should I do?"

Priest touched her shoulder and replied, "I know what a giving and loving spirit you are, but I ask you to think about what it is you are learning from your crisis with this man. What is different about him? Meditate on that question and the answer will come to you. Then you must pray for strength because you will need it."

He told her where he was staying and then said he had to go. Her eyes followed him as he exited. He opened the door as two men entered. It was her father and a man with no name that her father would later call Blackops.

"Sara, I'm sorry we're so late. My secretary made a mistake. I wanted us to meet at a place called The Healthy Soul and Margaret mixed up 8842 with 4882. So when I didn't hear from you, I checked with her and here we are."

Sara smiled to herself. *There are no coincidences*, she thought. "Senator, perhaps we were supposed to be here," she said.

Townsend was accustomed to her ethereal comments and paid no attention to her response. "I have news about Clint."

Blackops looked around. He felt safe talking here and made a note to himself to use this bar for discreet meetings in the future. Blackops told Sara about Jake and how Jake knew Clint. He told her about Clint's childhood, the secret program and told her that Clint was assigned to an assassination right now. They told her everything except the name of the target. Sara knew a great deal about Clint's past but some of what Blackops told her was new. She was deeply concerned for Clint because she knew that he was no longer a killer. They must be forcing him do this. This job would feel like a rape of his conscience. He must be in agony.

The meaning of Priest's appearance was now clear to Sara. Hurting as she was for Clint and as deeply as she empathized with his pain, Clint was a supremely gifted version of the Clone presence. He could elaborate on his suffering, protect himself, even occasionally kill his master. Not so for the 2 million other Clones, such as the domestic sex slaves living as targets for the frustration of any family. What of the Worker Clones forced to work in the fields for 18-hour shifts until they dropped from exhaustion and disease?

But worst of all, what about the Angels? These were Clones who were breast fed and dined on the finest organic foods. They were raised to be healthy athletic specimens in safe and tranquil environments, requirements of their wealthy customers.

When a request came in for an organ, the handsome Angel Clone was strapped to a table; the organs were crudely removed and carefully salvaged. The body was thrown quivering and bloody into the pit below.

In the pit the stench of the dead and the screams of the living were overwhelming. But to the discerning ear, the scraping of fingernails against rock was also audible, continuous and eerie. The Clones tried desperately to climb over each other to make their way to the top. They bit, clawed, pounded and killed each other to ascend a yard. Those few that made it were beheaded by guards and flung back into the pile, their necks gushing blood into the frightened eyes of the climbers below.

There were few naturally born men who could endure causing this daily suffering, so the "Doctors" and the guards were all Clones themselves.

Every five days a truck brought acid and dumped it into the hole before sealing it. A new pit was then dug by Worker Clones and the processing continued. Clint has wondered if Clones have souls, these Clones wonder if men do.

"Sara, you haven't said much. Did you know about any of this?"

She looked cautiously at Blackops and her Dad noticed. Townsend thanked him for his help and dismissed him. He nodded to Sara and Townsend and left.

As soon as he was out of sight Townsend said, "Sara, did you know about any of this"?

"Yes, Dad."

The Senator was astounded. "How could you befriend someone like that? He kills people for a living!"

"Dad, I saw killers at Dr. Benson's party. Those men are responsible for the deaths of tens of thousands and you sip champagne and laugh with these murderers. How to you do it?"

"Sara, it's not the same. I worry about you."

She saw that he meant it and she loved him for that. She leaned over and kissed him on the cheek. "Dad, I don't want to argue with you, but the guys at Dr. Benson's party have no conscience. They and their followers see only their goals. They negate the humanity of their enemies, so they can bomb them. They glorify the sacrifice of our troops so they can sacrifice them. They have no personal struggles, no inner dialogues, just master plans. Yes Clint was a killer, but he is far superior to your friends because he has remorse."

"Carmen, I mean Sara, are you in danger?"

Sara smiled. "No, Dad, he loves me, or at least I'm pretty sure he does. I know he would never harm me. That's why I am concerned. If he were OK, he would find me. If he were acting under his own free will he would be here, but he's not, so I worry."

Townsend said, "His target is very important and you're right, they are probably watching him. Is there anything you can tell me that might help us?

She looked at him and said, "He doesn't want to do it."

Chapter 9

Walt had driven to Washington to meet Sewell. Things were horrible in his neighborhood and, as far as he was concerned, all over the country. He felt helpless, just like the nation's people he had no voice. Norman was the only person he knew who was influential enough to change things. He couldn't let ego stand in the way. Black people were dying at four times the rate of whites and with limited resources were dying more and more. The only thing the government was inclined to offer Blacks or the poor were programs like the Reverend's.

As far as business was concerned, he remembered his Grandfather saying that Negro's needed to stick together and have an economic focus like the Jews who owned the apartment buildings and stores in Black neighborhoods. Then he remembered when his father said that Blacks need to work together like the Koreans who owned the small businesses in Harlem. As a young adult, his nephews' friends talked about the Mexicans who were taking jobs from Arican-Americans.

Then came gentrification. It was sickening to see others getting paid amazing sums for the small businesses that the locals patronized and rented, buildings that were then sold for millions by others to new corporate owners. Will the next generation be complaining about Clones owning businesses and taking away jobs. These trends, in Walt's opinion, had to stop.

We, as Black Americans, have to stop going into debt for what we want, Walt thought, *and start saving and investing for what we need.* Walt understood the whole personal responsibility thing. He knew the "I Have A Dream' speech but he also knew Dr. King advised his followers to start credit unions and to pool their resources. Dr. King began with a bus boycott in Alabama and his life ended while in Memphis fighting for Union rights. In between he started Operation Breadbasket which created millions of dollars of income in Black communities. *It's all economics,* Walt thought and his buddy was the chief advisor on economics in the country and a friend of the President. He just needed to help Norm get his mind set right.

Black men like him somehow forgot about the Homestead Act, which gave land to whites just before the beginning of the 20th century but excluded Blacks. They forgot that America's middle class got it's genesis from the G.I. Bill. Banks changed mortgages from 5 years to 30 years. Government introduced the GED so factory workers and farmers could go to college and then paid for their college tuition.

Most importantly, single-family houses were built from sea to shining sea to sell to the returning G.I.s. This led to the equity that created money for their kids to go to college and a financial base from which to prosper. Blacks, by federal law and bank policy were redlined and forbidden from buying these properties. Instead they gave Blacks federal housing projects, no ownership, and no economic strength.

Union salaries paid the best wages, but many refused to accept Blacks as members. So for centuries white laborers did not have to compete with Blacks. Affirmative Action, a policy that said that for centuries of free labor, rape, murder, the stealing of children from their parents and the dreams of a people, we will give you a few slots in education and employment.

But that wasn't fair to them. Imagine. Only the most clear white entitlement would allow someone to equate centuries of brutality with denial of a few job and work slots.

If the tables were turned, would White America want to experience such injustices, or just ten percent? How ludicrous is it for a Black man to defend a delusional construct that leaves Whites guiltless and Blacks penniless?

Walt knew he had to reach Norm and make him see his point of view. Norm was a good guy, but he just never fit in. He didn't know how to have fun and took the teasing of other children way too seriously. So in his mind, that made Blacks defective and each kid that didn't do well in school or got hooked on drugs supported his theory.

He went to college and did fantastic academically. He didn't fit in much better with Whites but he expected more and noticed less. Besides, where else was he going to go? He still talked to everyone in the neighborhood but his visits became more infrequent. Walt guessed partly because of his own modest success and partly because of all the times he saved Norm's ass, he was his only remaining friend from home.

"Dr Sewell will see you now."

"Walt, how are you doing, buddy?" Norm chose to ignore the fireworks of their last meeting. He had worked 14-hour days involved with the plot to assassinate the President and was physically exhausted and emotionally drained.

So when his childhood rescuer called, he felt safer, more relaxed, a sort of mood congruity. He was even toying with the idea of revealing the crisis to Walt and why not. Men of his stature had trusted advisors, confidantes. Hell, wasn't that why the President entrusted him with this? It certainly wasn't an economic matter. Yeah, Walt might be just the one, if friendship and this mission were enough to make him see beyond his politics.

"Come with me." Sewell took him to the safe room with the peeling paint. He entered the anteroom where they were scanned by several devices; a flashing light indicated there were listening devices present. He looked immediately at Walt with a look of astonishment and disappointment, and said, "What have you done?"

Walt had no idea what was going on. He reflexively stepped back when the Secret Service men approached. They came toward him with guns drawn and yelled for him to put his hands behind his head and drop to his knees.

Norm was mortified. As he interlocked his fingers and dropped to his knees, he looked to Walt for help. Their eyes locked before Norman turned away. When he did, Norm saw the flashing digital image of their two silhouettes, and digital arrows pointed to the presence of three bugs. The arrows were all on him. He motioned to the Secret Service men to look at the screen.

The Secret Service man that had been talking on his walkie-talkie said to Walt, "Get up, sir. I need you both to come with me."

Daniel Bloom was waiting in the big pivoting chair in the center of the Security Command Center in the White House. Men and women at the Command Center watched monitors, reviewed videos and received feedback from motion detectors, heat sensors and walkie-talkies. He was watching Sewell approach from the hallway monitor. He thought about how he had had Sewell bugged from the beginning.

He knew of his meeting with Townsend before Norman told him and knew Walt was coming. He knew when he was arriving and he knew more facts about Walt now than anyone except his mother. He knew he was Norman's rescuer and he knew Norman needed rescuing. He had watched how Sewell responded to the pace and intensity of this mission and found him lacking. He was the effete, intellectual with no substance, no gut and no heart.

All the Secret Service reports and his history indicated Walt was different. His passion for his principles did not stop at his throat. He was brave, disciplined and smart. But Bloom wanted to test his theory, so he had the Secret Service draw their weapons on Walt even though he knew Walt had done nothing wrong. He wanted to bring back Walt's memory of vulnerability when his friend was beaten and shot by police. He wanted to remind him of his moment of helplessness and humiliation and then look into his eyes and see what was there.

As for Norman, Blackops or those wanting to kill the President would be used as the reason for the bugs. Sewell was in over his head, anyway. He might be smart enough to think Bloom might be lying but not wise enough to know it.

Sewell and Walt entered. The bugs had been removed. Sewell looked weak and his voice was slightly high-pitched.

"Daniel, someone bugged me. Do we know who it was?"

Daniel listened.

Sewell got more emotional; he was sweating slightly and his voice cracked. He looked at Walt, who had taken a chair and was calmly watching everyone's response.

Yeah, Daniel thought, *I was right. Walt is a throwback. He's like those Blacks who faced guns, dogs and death in the Civil Rights movement. But Norman ,he thought, is all video games and buttered popcorn.* Daniel said, "Don't worry, Norman, everything will be all right."

"Walter is it?"

"Yes," Walt said.

"I need to speak to Norman alone, Walter. Roberts will escort you back to Mr. Sewell's office."

"Norman, have a seat," Daniel said. "I know this has been trying for you and you have shown real leadership. The President showed good insight in selecting you and you are a good friend to him. It's unfortunate that you have been compromised. You may have been bugged for some other reason but we have to be safe, buddy. We must assume that it is the same guys who are trying to murder the President. I will tell the President how hard you worked but you must now take a lesser role in this fight since you are being watched. Maybe we can use you as a decoy."

Sewell made a mild protest but accepted Bloom's story. You could see him unburdening. By the end of their short conversation, he was sitting up straight in his chair and his voice and bearing had returned. He shook Bloom's hand and left.

As Sewell walked to his office his pep and vigor had returned. He thought that maybe one day he would tell Walt about the assassination plot but not today. He opened the door to his outer office and smiled at his secretary as he walked by and opened the door. He entered his office and looked around for his friend, but Walt was gone.

Chapter Ten

Sara called Priest the day after seeing him in the Clone Bar. She told him that she knew she wanted to work for the liberation of the Clones. She would take time away from being a Healer and her assistants and students would temporarily handle her pro bono healing. Money would be tight, so she would continue to provide services to her wealthy customers.

Sara always felt that Clones were human because a small segment of her patients were Clones. She helped them with herbs and potions, but she also helped them with spiritual healing. And you have to have a spirit to be spiritually healed. Yet for so many people this did not prove anything.

Men had made great strides technologically but were mere babies in understanding their inner selves. Soulless Clones would certainly symbolize the focus on the flesh at the expense of the spirit; the triumph of rationality over imagination. She remembered how the ancients taught philosophy and science together as twin pillars of understanding.

In fact, it is philosophy that is both the father of science and a child of God. Had the Kings and Priests allowed this natural way to continue, our spirits would be able to travel to distant galaxies and our people would not go hungry.

Sara arrived before Priest and meditated in the park. When she opened her eyes she saw him sitting beside her. She smiled. "How long have you been sitting there?"

"Not long. I did not want to disturb you," Said Priest. "You look relaxed. I think you have found your answer."

Sara said, "I need your help."

Priest responded, "We have only one need, the rest are wants. What do you want?"

"I want to reduce the suffering of the Clones."

Priest said, "There are only two ways to reduce mass suffering, either by promoting justice or by teaching acceptance. Which will you do?"

Her answer came quickly. "Promote justice."

He smiled. "You have chosen the path of prophets. To achieve justice you must confront power, challenge institutions and endure the hatred of the crowd. You must change them while loving them.

"You must see their beauty oozing through their ignorance like water trickling through a dam. You must speak from your light to their light."

"I want to help them. I did not say I wanted to lead," Sara said.

"Your spirit, your form is magnetic and your energy is electric. You are the fire for change. You still have choice but if you choose this path, you will lead one day."

Sara now felt that all the major moments of her life had brought her to this instant, to the edge of this cliff. She did not know whether splendid flight or certain death would be the consequence of her leap. But it all seemed familiar and necessary.

She looked into Priest's eyes with intense certainty and said, "Let's begin."

"OK, come with me," Priest replied.

Priest had been working with the Replica Resistance. These were Clones that were different. Each had qualities or defects that allowed them to resist their initial programming and think freely. Some had through error or beneficence escaped the frontal lobe operation. All were first generation Clones. They matured realizing that they were different and most chose to hide their ability from the world. They realized that if either humans or Clones knew, they would have them programmed or used for low-end spare parts. They did not long to be human like so many other Clones. In fact many had a hard time distinguishing between humans and Clones, since most humans they met behaved as though they were programmed.

The Replica Resistance grew their organization one member at a time. They slowly and carefully identified new potential members. At the time their leader was introduced to Sara, they had 7,000 free thinkers in their movement.

Priest described this history to Sara. She was eager to help and fascinated with the movement's origins. Priest's words interrupted her thoughts. "We are almost there."

Sara looked around. They were descending a winding road, which ended near the beach. A dome-shaped building could be seen in the distance. She let down the window to enjoy the breeze. The wind made her hair dance. It was a beautiful day.

The dome was larger than it had looked from a distance. Although it appeared large enough to hold hundreds, no one seemed to be there. She thought maybe cars were parked on the other side. They entered the building after Priest inserted a card and uttered a series of numbers and phrases. They walked down a long hall passing offices and classrooms. They passed two grand ballrooms. They walked through one of them and then through an empty kitchen.

They made a right turn and arrived at a long hallway. At the end of the hallway was a door and a narrow stairway. The stairs led to a huge cavern with tiny streams of water and eclectic colors. The water zigzagged around unique rock formations--speeding, slowing, descending, then colliding at the bottom with oncoming waves that force water up against the cave wall and then rejoins the great mass of water that races to the shore.

Sara carefully proceeded down the steps, placing her hand against the cave wall for balance. She loved the rush of the water and the sound of the birds, so carefree and melodic. As she descended farther another sound intruded. Whatever it was disturbed the awesome serenity she felt. She was at the bottom now and edged along the wall, avoiding the vibrant passage of water escaping from deep within the cave. Priest stepped lightly and quickly for an older man; she felt like she was holding him back. Now the intruding sound echoed and reverberated all around her. It was the voices of men; it was the voices of Clones.

A few Clones who were standing at the edge of the crowd turned and looked at them as they joined the assembly. They were probably security. They nodded at Priest and instantly returned their eyes to the front. The crowd was huge and mesmerized by the speaker. They would roar with laughter or with ferocity depending on how he moved them. Sara stood on tip-toes and stretched her neck so she could catch a glimpse of him. She excused herself as she made her way through the crowd. She ducked in between some, turned her body sideways and squeezed by others. The audience was tightly packed. Every time she arrived at the place she thought she could see better, she was still staring at heads and backs. So she decided to just focus on his voice. The speaker's voice was clear, moving and familiar.

"They say we have no history; we say we are timeless. They say we do not belong: we say we have no boundaries. They say we have no credibility; we say we have no limitations. They say they are few; we say we are one.

"We will no longer look to others to support our cause. We will define ourselves and we will protect ourselves. We thought that those who have felt the misery of oppression, the lie of dehumanization, would support us. We thought that they would see that common suffering was more important than our differences.

"Instead they wanted to feel superior. The once illegal immigrants, Gays, Blacks, even Native Americans treated us like filth, or ,at best, like pets.

"No, we must lead the fight because the foot of injustice is closest to our neck. The others live in shit and the government tells them it is roses. When they bleed they think they have been pricked by thorns. They suffer and continue to proclaim the beauty of the rose.

"The religious community justifies our genocide by calling our existence a sin. I wonder if stealing a man's emotions with brain operations is a sin? I wonder if using my beating heart to prolong their greedy, decadent lives is a sin? I wonder if being killed as a soldier, defending a land where I have no rights and no hope is a sin?

"We are the new guardians of ideals of truth, justice and freedom. We know the true meaning of these words because there are times when their energy is all we have to sustain us.

"The rich use these words to make fools of the masses. They seek to gut the soul from these words and replace their meaning with marketable counterfeits.

"The true church struggles against a well-financed, well connected distortion of Jesus. The media values ratings above integrity; these traditional allies of truth and liberty are bought and paid for. So what do we do against such overwhelming odds?

"We resolve to become masters of our own thoughts. We must resist the globalization of conformity. We must become philosophers and thinkers. We must have beginners' minds.

"We must live truth even if it is hard and fight evil even though it is strong. Our ideals must vanquish our fears.

"My mind is clear and so is my heart. It is why I am here today to fight for justice for Replicas. It is why I am here today to fight for the minds of men."

As the crowd erupted with deafening approval, Sara tugged at Priest's garment. Cupping her hand and placing it on his ear, she yelled, "It's Clint, it's Clint. I recognize his voice!"

Priest said, "He is not the one you seek. As soon as I can I will introduce you."

Sara was almost certain, and her heart was beating quickly. "Can we hurry?"

She grabbed Priest's hand and moved through the crowd. The closer they moved the more tightly packed the crowd became until they couldn't move anymore. Sara looked in both directions anxiously.

Priest said, "Sara, it is almost impossible to get to him now. I know where he will be tonight. I will arrange for us to meet with him."

Sara looked disappointed but acknowledged the hopelessness of seeing him right away.

The hours passed slowly but Sara's face brightened as Priest announced, "Only a couple of minutes now."

They arrived at a nondescript house in a suburb of Baltimore.

Someone unlocked the door and shouted, "I'm in a towel. Please come in and relax. I'll be there in a minute."

Sara looked at Priest and thought, *What kind of weird game is this? That is Clint's voice!*

They walked to the living room; Priest seemed to know his way around. Sara looked for clues of the leader's personality by searching for books and artwork. She saw none, only bare walls and neutral colors. If this place were to burn, if he lost everything, he lost nothing.

They sat down. The Replica leader emerged in a bathrobe. He was drying his hair with a towel and descending the steps. Sara stretched her neck to glimpse his full face.

He entered the living room, holding both ends of the towel around his neck. "Sorry for the delay but after a long day, I get in the shower and get lost in my thoughts." He moved toward Sara. "Hi, I'm Paul."

She took his hand in a timid and removed way, like it was a murder weapon she was obligated to identify. All the while her eyes cascaded over his body. She had not let go of his hand. He placed his other hand over hers, gently removing the first and said, "Priest has told me that you are a remarkable person." He said "person" hoping to have his mind avoid what an incredibly beautiful woman she was.

"H-hi, I'm sorry but you look so much like a friend of mine, you even sound like him." She managed a weak smile.

Paul responded, "Well, I can't vouch for your friend's character but he sounds like a great looking guy." He had hoped for a smile. Paul sat down and he and Priest reacquainted themselves.

As they talked Sara concluded that this was not Clint playing some cruel joke but a man so remarkably like him that he could be his brother, if not his twin. He was chubbier, less muscled, younger and less dark than Clint. Despite his leadership position in this outlawed organization, this was a man who smiled often. This was a man who would meet someone for the first time in his bathrobe.

Still, his resemblance made Sara think about Clint at a depth that she had avidly avoided. She felt suddenly uncomfortable and asked Paul, "Is it ok if I take a short walk? I need some air."

Paul said, "Sure."

Priest asked to accompany her and started to get up, but she waved him off and headed for the door. She was about to pass the high hedges that surrounded the house when she was grabbed from behind. She started to scream but a hand was placed instantly over her mouth. She was quickly lowered to the lawn. She continued to try to scream or to wriggle out of his grasp. She wondered if the person was going to rape her. Was it the Black Hummers again?

Her assailant whispered, "Shhhh." He turned her around so that she was facing him. He cradled her in his lap. It was Clint.

"Sara, I've missed you so much."

She pulled him to her and hugged him tightly. Her eyes filled with tears of joy. "Where have you been?"

Two men watched Sara disappear. They were in a house across the street and their job was to protect Paul. They were Replica Resistance's equivalent of the Secret Service.

As they approach, Clint hears them. He asks Sara to get up and see who they are. She does and begins telling them that she twisted her ankle and begins limping away from the lawn. One of them moves to assist her, and the other starts moving in the direction she came from, towards Clint. She stumbles deliberately and more emphatically, begging the other security man for assistance. He ignores her and continues searching. Using a walkie-talkie, he calls Paul. "Sir, could you turn on the floodlights."

As security moves closer, Clint surprises and disarms him. The guard with Sara hears the rustling of the hedges. He quickly moves away from Sara, calls Paul and warns, "Sir, please stay inside."

Too late. Paul and Priest are both outside when, seconds later, the floodlights come on. Sara runs back to where she last saw Clint.

The security guard turns quickly with his weapon held high. "Move back, miss."

Sara stops instantly.

The guard feels his legs buckle beneath him. His face hits the ground and before his head bounces up, it is pinned by Clint's knee. Clint grabs his hand and twists his arm behind him at a 90 degree angle, causing him to drop his weapon. Clint retrieves the weapon and motions for the other security guard to move toward Paul and Priest, who he looks at for the first time. They are on the porch and have been watching without moving, everything having occurred faster than they could respond. Clint places a hand above his eyes trying to avoid the glare of the floodlights.

His eyes move first to their hands and he sees they have no weapons; their stances indicates that they are not prepared to act. He moves out of the glare.

"Walk towards me so I can see you better. Sara, please come stand beside me." He takes her hand and she begins to whisper than these are friends. He does not hear her, he sees only Paul. He drops her hand and drops the gun. They stare at each other.

"Me2," Clint says and they embrace.

Chapter Eleven

The Kingmaker's associates felt it all slipping away. Yet they were still required to provide him with a status report. Mr. Dour Renfield gave his report from the field. "Desertions are increasing and so are demonstrations against the wars."

"What are you doing about it?" the Kingmaker interrupted.

"We are instructing commanders in the field to shoot deserters. We are requiring all available troops to watch these firing squads, which we hope will act as a deterrent to others that might think about deserting."

The representative from the State Dept. Conny McMammi spoke. "We have strengthened our agreements with Canada and Mexico for extradition of draft dodgers escaping to those countries. Mexico has complained about the number of illegal U.S. immigrants fleeing to their country. Imagine."

"Continue, Dour", the Kingmaker said.

Conny sat down.

"There have been demonstrations all over the country but the biggest ones are in New York and Washington D.C. We have declared all the protesters Enemy Combatants. We have used the Tribunals to put the organizers away. The problem is that new organizers keep popping up. Oh, we also used the Military Commissions Act to warn that those who donate to organizations that oppose the war can be made Enemy Combatants as well. This should cut off funding to these organizations."

"What about the press, Snowjob?"

Tony Snowjob responded, "Yes sir, the heads of both media conglomerates are supporting our efforts. There are no pictures of the anti-war, anti-draft demonstrations. They are focusing on entertainment and minimizing serious stories. They present our point of view. Wolf News continues to encourage good citizens to identify these traitors. The Internet was the only form of mass communication these people had but with the end of the "Common Carrier" laws, we can eliminate any group's ability to get their messages through on the Internet."

"Good, good. What about money, is there any good news?"

Everyone put their heads down; they knew what was coming. It had been decided during the past year that no one person would have the responsibility of reporting on the dismal financial outlook, so they rotated. It was Renfield's turn.

"Well, as you know, the stock market's doing fine. The corporations that we control or have hidden interests in have enough money to start small countries. We pass on these tremendous estates without paying any taxes and make people with no real wealth finance the country and pay us for our services."

There were some restrained smiles at the table. Rennie was stating the obvious as a prelude to the bad news.

The Kingmaker just glared at him. "OK, because of the wars we owe China, Japan and Saudi Arabia one trillion dollars. We have a huge trade imbalance with every country we do business with, the dollar is in serious trouble and OPEC is threatening to move to the Euro. If we don't change course, there will be nothing left to take."

Everyone was silent. All you could hear was the rustling of papers.

The Kingmaker stood up, placed his hands on the long table, looked around and said, "Look, I know things sound bleak but remember that we wanted to get rich and now we are wealthier than any people in the history of the world. We and our friends have looted the treasury and are totally innocent of any crime. They gave it to us. It's been better than winning jackpots in Las Vegas.

"Now we cannot regret that the source that enriched us is gone. We have to find a way to replenish the pot. The opposition party will have to raise taxes, make trade tariffs that favor American workers, reduce the debt and make policies that increase wages. People will have more to spend. This should bring more money into the pot. If there were some catastrophic event that brought the country together--against an internal enemy say--we could exploit their patriotism again and rob them blind. I think the Clones are great for this purpose. They have no rights and no one cares about them. We could exaggerate the threat of existing Clone resistance groups and make one of their leaders like Osama. We could let him live in captivity while we create threatening messages allegedly from him, keeping the people in fear and dependent on us to protect them.

"Finally, as the minority party with tons of capital and political infrastructure, we could attack them for their weakness at every opportunity. This approach promises to lead us to victory in next election and we will thrive once more."

They knew he was the man to do it. He had been successful so many times before. They were pleased with the overall plan but had questions.

"Let's meet again in a couple of weeks and talk about this in more detail," the Kingmaker insisted.

After they left, the new Vice President arrived. Lon Chaney was asked to be a running mate by the new President. The Democratic Innocuous Council (DIC's) thought having a Vice President from the other party would help heal the country and get more independent and moderate opposition voters to vote for them. They were right.

"Sit down, Lon, or should I say Mr. President?"

Lon smiled and greeted the Kingmaker warmly.

"The beauty of this thing, Lon, is that the shooter looks exactly like the Replica Resistance leader. I shit you not. So the world will see this guy shoot the President. The actual leader, a guy named Paul, will go to a place at the shore to hide. We will send our people there to get him.

"Lon, you will lead the nation in its wars against our internal and external enemies, while their Congress replenishes our treasury. Priceless"

As the two men left, they felt confident in their plan and wondered why they were ever worried at all.

II

Daniel Bloom had sensed something special about Walt and sought to deputize him, the way they did in the old west. Daniel was rarely impulsive but valued his instincts, and the plan had called for an unknown. He needed someone who was smart and brave and definitely not with the other side. He took Walt to the special room. Walt knew he wanted something; he just didn't have a clue what it was. They sat down.

"Walt, you have been in a few of those antiwar and anti-draft demonstrations, right?"

"Is that a problem?" Walt responded.

"No. You've even spoken at a couple of them, haven't you?"

"Yeah, and I would do it again," Walt replied.

"Good. That's what I have in mind. The President will be speaking at a university in Virginia. He will surprise the nation by announcing his plans to begin withdrawal of troops from Iraq and then a phased withdrawal from the other two fronts."

"That's great news! A lot of lives will be saved," Walt said with enthusiasm.

"Yes, but as you might imagine, there are people who profit in many ways from the war: It makes it very dangerous for the President, his enemies would not like him to make this speech."

Walt looked at Daniel quizzically. It sounded like he was saying the President was in danger. "Is there some way I can help?"

Daniel thought about giving him the grateful nation speech but concluded that he was already motivated, and motivated for the right reasons. "Walt, when the President speaks, he does not like to have a lot of Secret Service people on stage. Also, any potential conspirators have been watching us and will probably know who our people are. Because of the nature of the President's speech, we can use your anti-war experience to place you on the stage as an unknown quantity."

"I'm not trained, what if...?"

Daniel interrupts. "What if you get shot? What if you save the President? What if nothing happens? We don't know. I only know we need you and I think you want to help. Should I insult you by offering you money?"

Walt understood what Daniel meant by this. Anyone who would risk his life on this grand scale, did not do it for money. If he and the President didn't die, this might give him the access to the President he wanted, with or without Norm. But what Walt said was, "Please insult me. How much money are we talking about?"

Daniel said, "$500,000."

"With the dollar shrinking the way that it is, I'll need my eyeglasses to see that. I'll do it for $750,000."

"Deal," Daniel said and shook his hand.

Walt was pleased to have the money. It would help out at home. The two men smiled knowing that Walt could have held out for more and would have done it for nothing.

"Let's get you trained; I understand you used to be a bit of an athlete."

Walt patted his stomach. "Yeah, a long time ago."

"Don't worry. The things you have to learn are more mental than physical and include such skills as observation, dissecting the crowd, recognizing anomalies, anticipation and communication. I have assigned you our best trainers.

"I remember that you like playing speed-Chess. Think of it like that:, focus, refocus, predict, plan, react. Each instant is powerful and irreversible."

Walt had a strange feeling, a feeling that was known only to a fortunate few. Sara felt this when she decided to help the Clones. It was the pinnacle of existence: knowing you must sacrifice your life at the moment you discover its purpose. Finding your path is like having a hundred orgasms at once. After knowing such incredible joy, can one risk ending all feeling?

Like horses chained to your wrist and moving in different directions, instinctual self-preservation and godly self-sacrifice vie for supremacy. You are stuck in a paradox. Until ultimately you realize that you can never return to life before that instant of knowing, it would be worse than death.

Walt wanted to experience this feeling privately and then talk to his family. He excused himself. Daniel wanted to get started right away. Walt insisted on the delay. He was sure that something tragic would happen. He felt so alive, he wanted have the joy of that. He wanted to say just the right words to his family, using playful and polite conversation to express his love for them and give advice for the future. He had to be careful not to let his devotion to them blunt his resolve.

Walt was feeling everything so intensely, the trees blowing in the wind, the sounds of children in the playground. He was seeing life vividly. Everything was slower and clearer, even his thoughts. He reveled in this heightened state. He wandered around feeling, touching and thinking, seeing everything as if for the first time. Feeling like he could emerge from his skin, he almost willed himself to do so, when his eye spotted a smiling little girl. She was so wonderful. She reminded him of his daughter. He realized that the best chance of returning home to his family required that he get all the training he could get. Why not put all this intensity to good use?

Walt picked up his cell phone. While looking at the picture of his family, which appeared when he flipped the phone open, he punched in a code that would scramble the call.

Daniel answered the call immediately. "Yes, Walt?"

Walt replied confidently, "I'm ready."

Chapter Twelve

Sara, Priest, Clint and Paul drive along in silence. They have shed all pens and electronic devices and Clint has checked their shoes for bugs. They are headed for a 24-hour car rental office. Sara pays in cash while the others wait. Once they are in the car, certain they will not be overheard, they begin to speak.

Sara begins. "Clint, did you find me or did you find Paul?"

Clint replies, "I thought Paul was dead."

Paul turns his head.

"Why?" Sara asks.

Clint responds, "When I was a child and realized that I would have no friends and no real family, I imagined that I had a brother. I would have imaginary conversations with him to relieve my loneliness. He was my playmate. A few years later when I realized what I was, I wanted to create the brother I had imagined. I asked the Colonel and he refused, but because so many of my counterparts were experiencing problems we all saw psychologists regularly. The chief psychologist decided that it might be good for me to have this as a project. As I had advanced intellect and access to the best Cloning information and scientists available, I created Paul."

Sara is astonished. "But you told me that the survival rate for second generation Uberclones is only 10%. How did he survive?"

"Well, what the human cloners didn't know is that Clones of Clones have more insight into what their 'offspring' is feeling, and with my enhanced intuitive qualities, I was a great mother. I was also a fair scientist."

Paul looks at Clint sternly. "Yeah, but not too good a brother." He sees a momentary hurt expression on Clint's face and responds gently "But you made up for it later," Paul assures him.

Clint acknowledges Paul's pain. "He's right. Although I wanted love so badly, they were breeding a killer. They cultivated negative emotions in me. I must confess that in my darker moments I wanted to treat someone with the distain that I was treated with. I hated them but I identified with their power."

Priest says, "Yet you embraced the moment you saw each other."

Clint looks at Sara, his eyes seeking assurance that this stranger belongs in this most private of conversations.

She pulls him close and whispers, "He is like a father to me. He has my complete trust."

Clint, while locked in eye contact with Priest, continues, "I was damaged. Paul experienced a roller coaster of needy affection and demeaning criticism. But he is the reason I became the best. They used visits with him as a reward for good conduct and performance. I always wanted to see Paul, so I excelled.

"Things changed after I went to college. I was 17 and Paul was 8. He would go into town and to the college. He made friends easily and tried to share them with me. Despite all my anger and aggression, we bonded. He became my teacher. Then in my Junior year, which was the best year of my life, the Colonel decided that Paul was making me too soft, too caring. The next thing I knew Paul had disappeared. I didn't see him ever again until today."

Sara's eyes well up with tears; so do Paul's.

Clint turns and for the first time in many years looks directly at Paul and asks affectionately, "So, brother, where have you been?"

Paul replies, "You are right, Clint. They did come for me, but I was warned, inadvertently. Remember how I used to enjoy learning your college level classes, mostly Physics and Psychology?"

"Yeah, you were a little pest with that stuff, always thinking you were smarter than me." The memory makes Clint smile.

"Well, I was recording one of your online classes when I received a call saying that one of my friends and his parents had been in a car accident. I rushed out. I left the computer and the recording device on. They came in while I was gone. When I got back, I got something to eat and returned to the computer. I replayed the recording and I could hear their voices in the room. It was clear what they wanted to do to me. I packed some clothes and I left."

Clint is upset by this revelation. "Why didn't you leave me a note?"

"I did, but you were away on a training exercise. They must have taken it. I tried to reach you many times after that but I never got a response."

Clint says, "When I couldn't find you I rebelled. I refused to go to training exercises or participate in any way until they brought you back. They tried to convince me that you had been hit by a bus and showed me photos of you bleeding and mangled. They even had a news story inserted in the local paper but I didn't believe them. They drugged me, tortured me and had their best psychologist convince me that I was in denial from grief over losing you. Little by little I accepted their story. I closed myself off and decided not to care again. I became the weapon they longed for. I had no feelings until I met Sara."

Sara asks Paul, "Where did you go after discovering they wanted to kill you?"

"The first thing I did was get rid of everything in my wallet. I even asked a friend of Clint's to make a call from my cell phone when he went home for break and then to mail my cell phone to another friend in another state and ask him to make a call. I told them I was playing a joke on someone. I did this to throw them off my trail.

"I ended up on the west coast where a Mexican family took me in. They were migrant farm workers. We got up very early in the morning and ate cornmeal or oatmeal for breakfast. On a good day we had a piece of bacon. We picked relentlessly until our arms could no longer lift. Planes flew overhead covering the sky with insecticide, which poisoned the rain that poured into the vats of drinking water. We saw the filmy rainbow in the tainted water but it was the only water available to drink. We put bandanas over our cups to filter the water. We drank and we prayed. If not for your special genes, brother, I would probably be dead from cancer."

Clint feels true pain at the description of Paul's suffering and partially blames himself for it.

"How long were you there?" he asks.

"Not long," Paul says. "About three years. We moved around a lot and no one came looking for me. I guess I was away from you and that's what they wanted."

Sara asks, "What happened next?"

Paul is slow to answer. He can see the hurt expression on Clint's face. "How about if we skip forward a little bit? This is a story for another time. Let me tell you how I met Priest."

Clint starts to object. He wants to know more about Paul's life, painful or not. He does not protest, however, because he is interested in knowing more about this person who has so affected Sara and Paul, the people he cares about most.

Paul begins, "We met at the home of the philanthropist Warren Turner Gates. WTG was a man who had the ability to instantly immerse himself in achievement. He lived most of his life like a man playing a video game, excited by the unexpected, making the right move at just the right time and totally absorbed by the game. It was no surprise that he rose quickly and remained at the top of his field. Others thought he was a white-collar executioner; he saw himself as just better at the game than they were. He invested wisely, choosing to invest in the things he knew best and thoroughly analyzing the companies he selected. He loved communication, movies, the Internet, cell phones and TV. He had achieved the pinnacle of financial success when he met Priest.

"Priest introduced him to a greater pleasure than making money: the joy of giving it away. Priest knew that WTG would become the world's greatest philanthropist. It was not because WTG suddenly thought he had too much money or experienced a lifechanging event. It was that he craved the excitement of the game and he wanted to win. The old game had lost much of its excitement. He knew the players, he knew what to expect and he had won dozens of times. Priest introduced him to a new way of thinking at which he was a novice. This soul-work required that he start from the bottom. He became totally immersed in the new game.

"Priest helped to initiate the new thinking, the redirection of his energy. Priest knew how deep WTG's conviction had become. In the greatest evidence of his transformation, WTG had to choose between becoming the world's richest man or giving away millions, assuring that he would not. He gave it away. Many other wealthy men and women followed in his footsteps. It was a transcendent moment a victory of the spirit and a death to the ego that resulted in immense pleasure.

"He would later create the largest foundation in the world. His mission was to cure disease and fight hunger. He was succeeding on a grand scale."

Priest had been flown out two days before the gathering and was a guest at his home. Priest adds, "When great and powerful men know giving, they send ripples through the universe."

There is a short silence before Sara asks Paul, "Why were you there?"

"I had already begun to do some organizing. There were seven of us spread out around the country. It was difficult, but we communicated every day. Almost all of us worked grueling jobs. John, a fellow organizer, and I lived here and found colleges with huge lecture halls and sat in on classes. If we got caught we changed schools. That is how we got our education.

"While sitting in on a Law class, I met WTG's son. He had failed the bar twice and was auditing classes at the Law School to brush up. This was before WTC's enlightenment. His son blamed Capitalism for all the wrongs in the world and his father was one of the world's most successful Capitalists. He worked for the poor by day and partied with the rich at night. He occasionally befriended a few of his impoverished clients and brought them into his circle. It made him look really counter-culture and his guests got access to more drugs.

"Eventually I trusted him enough to discuss the Replica Resistance movement. He was immediately interested and wanted to do something to help. He became our benefactor and paid for the other members of our group to come join us. He supplied us with money for housing and expenses. Our group began to grow.

"He was becoming more and more reckless though and we selfishly began asking for bigger sums of money because we didn't know if he would be around for very long. This was troubling his father too. I learned that his father initially found Priest as a last ditch effort to save his son. WTG was a rational man who didn't believe in any of that 'spiritual shit', as he called it, but he was a desperate father. He would ask Priest for updates on his son and the two began to talk."

Priest interrupts. "I did not do that much. Once his father became more spiritual and giving, his son changed. He became a Capitalist. He passed the Bar, stopped his activity with the poor and became an activist for the rich. He even promoted an effort for the rich to hoard their wealth. It was called 'Kill the Death Tax'. It seems all he really wanted to do was to rebel against whatever his father was."

Paul smiles. "Yeah, Priest really blew it for us. In fact, the time that I met Priest at WTG's house was almost the last time I saw WTG'S son. He invited us back three more times over the next year. Each time he was more and more distant. We became concerned he might even turn us over to the authorities, so we changed our housing, changed our identities and never had anything to do with him again. Anyway, I was there for a couple of days before the gathering and Priest and I began to talk. He is the most evolved man I have ever known."

Clint looks at Sara who is nodding and beaming in her admiration for this man. Clint's jealousy arises but is doused by a wave of curiosity.

Clint thinks: *Who knows what will happen to me tomorrow? If I am not killed attempting to save the President, a secondary marksman will shoot me. I am pretty sure that was the plan even if I had made the hit. If I manage to survive tomorrow, Defense will make killing me their priority.*

So do I gamble on Priest's ability to explain the purpose of life or do I experience Sara, my life's greatest pleasure more fully and more intimately than I have ever known? Do I sacrifice the known for the unknown? Do I exchange the greatest pleasure of the senses for an elusive intangible joy?

Sara touches my hand and whispers, "Clint, I need to talk to you alone. I have been told some things."

He doesn't really hear what she says next. His eyes rest on her beauty, he loves the tone of her voice, the touch of her hand, the perfection of her body and her transcendent, ebullient spirit. *There is a glow to this woman, this surreal Madonna of true holiness and perfect form. I want her to bless me; I want her to fuck me. I am as ashamed of my thoughts as I am excited by them. There is a schism of my being. A man of two minds is unstable in all his ways.*

"Clint, are you listening to me?"

"Yes, Sara."

They stand looking into each other's eyes, suddenly oblivious to the other two. As Clint holds Sara's hand, his other hand is grabbed by Priest, who speaks not to him but to Sara.

"My dear, I will only keep him an hour or two, but there are things he must hear."

Sara has waited so long for answers, for intimacy, for balance, but she relents. Clint, who is undecided, submits to the certainty of Priests words.

"There are things he must hear."

Clint and Sara's hands slowly release their embrace. Clint decides not to look back.

"Come on," he barks at Priest.

Priest drives Clint away. They are both relatively quiet until they stop in front of a dilapidated roadside bar.

Priest says, "Follow me."

They enter the bar and immediately get looks from many in the crowd. They are both out of place here. Priest spots a table in the back and points towards it. The music blares loud and shrill. People speak loudly, some because of the volume of the music, others because of their character.

"What can I get cha?" the waitress asks. She takes the order, smiles at Clint and then rotates her hips through the crowd.

"Why are we here?" Clint asks.

"Wow, you get right to the heavy stuff," Priest says.

"No," says Clint, "I didn't mean why are we here on earth; I meant why are we here in this bar?"

Priest laughs. "I know what you meant. Actually the answer to both is the same: We are here to learn."

Clint says, "I thought that we would go to someplace isolated like a beach or a mountain or an empty church."

"That is where we go to see our ideal self; this is where we come to see who we are," Priest replies.

Clint looks around and sees four men arguing, one pounding the table and another whose neck muscles are clenched. He sees a woman with too much makeup and too short a dress, desperately seeking attention. She appears keenly aware of her fading beauty. He eyes several drunks, floating between despair and exhilaration. "I don't see any of myself in these people."

Priest says, "What I meant was that we can find ourselves in serene, peaceful environments but it is hard to maintain ourselves in our everyday routines." He hesitates a moment. "But Clint, are you saying that you see none of yourself in these people?

Clint scans the crowd again quickly. "I think you don't really know me. I am a disciplined guy. I don't drink or smoke, I exercise regularly, and I am pretty intelligent and worldly."

Priest responds, "I know a lot about you. In part, I agree with your assessment of yourself, but you have more in common with these people than you think."

"What do you mean?"

"They are so disappointed with the disparity between their true self and their actual life that they will accept almost anything to escape the pain of that disappointment."

Clint looks at him quizzically.

Priest continues, "Some take out their pain on themselves, use alcohol, drugs, gluttony, depression, ignorance; others abuse their children, spouses or employees or strangers. These are the obvious signs of pain.

"Others immerse themselves in positive things like exercise, discipline, work or materialism that often causes imbalance in their life and falsifies the true meaning of their existence. We build men of straw to keep the crows away and then we imagine the straw men are real."

Clint asks, "So what should we do?"

"I told you before," Priest says. "Learn".

"I don't have time for riddles, Priest," Clint says angrily. "Learn what?"

Priest says, "Learn about virtue and our innate goodness. It is the ultimate joy. The ego knows this. The ego's greatest fear is that we will be humiliated, impoverished or harmed by our selfless acts. Nations fear that we will not work to build their empires or fight in their armies. Families, thinking that they are acting in their children's behalf, facilitate the interests of the institutions and ideas that enslave them."

"Do you want anarchy"? Clint asks.

Priest continues, "If the society, the family and the ego act against ones interest, is it surprising that there are so few people who find the wisdom and courage to love virtue?"

Clint responds, "I think most people would like to be good and like the feeling of doing a good deed but you act like this is the secret of life and worth risking all the good we already have. Is that what you're saying?"

"I am saying that the kindness you speak of is like a calm lake. The virtue I speak of is like mighty waves that are damned by ignorance. Loving acts create holes in the dam. We become part of something stronger than the walls that confine us."

"You mean God," Clint says.

"Of course," Priest replies.

"So you're the expert, eh? Who is God."

"Do you mean is he a Muslim, Christian, Hindu, like that?" Priest asks.

"Yeah" Clint says. "Let's start there."

Priest bows his head momentarily and then looks up. "God is the energy and therefore the life in all things. He is the intelligence in our DNA and in gravity and is the beauty in art and poetry."

"Does he control our destiny?" Clint asks.

"We have millions of possible destinies, like the sperm that creates us and the stars in the galaxies. Only one is meant to hit its mark. The others we come to as a result of error, especially at the crossroads of our life. Yet even then, we remain drawn to our best destiny, like a salmon swimming upstream, but we do not always make it. If we learn enough, we do better next time."

"So you believe in reincarnation," Clint says. "Isn't that inconsistent with some religions?"

"No. The energy that is our spirit is neither created nor destroyed. There is still only one life, just many bodies."

"What about heaven and hell?" Clint asks.

"The soul lives a tragic, demon possessed existence when lost. Look around you."

He does and nods. Priest shakes his head in despair while scanning the crowd.

Priest says, "You know I can see demons; do you believe me?"

Clint shrugs his shoulders and asks, "What do they look like?"

Priest responds, "Much like you would expect. More important is where they are. They are on the shoulder or hovering above their victims, sometimes moving between victims. True hell is when the demons continue to attach themselves to victims after death. The human is now a spirit in the material world of demons. These are tragic souls."

Priest reflects for a moment and then looks at Clint. "Ask the question you really want to ask."

Clint looks at him intently and just as he begins to speak, the band starts to play its finale, the only hit it was ever known for. The crowd cheers in recognition and relives an idealized past. The lady with too much makeup pretends to adjust her skirt as she stands and cheers.

Clint shouts, "DO CLONES HAVE SOULS?"

"What you really want to know is, do you have a soul and if it has been condemned for the way you lived your life, right?"

"Yes."

"I know that you have given much thought to this question. What is in your heart and mind?"

Clint answers, "My mind tells me that the practice of any true religion would scorn my taking of life. The sheer enjoyment and pride I felt in killing made the act more reprehensible. I have too much Karma to pay back. I need forgiveness. My head tells me that I better be a Christian."

"There are belief systems that would allow you to live amorally. Would you like me to tell you about them?"

Clint glares at him. "I think that I will die soon. What I want to know is this: Am I a soulless being that is disconnected from God because I am man-made? If I do have a soul, how can I redeem myself before death? If you can help me with these things, I really need to know."

The crowd claps vigorously. Some embrace, others wipe sweat from their brows after the long dance, many look desperately around the room seeking a companion, hoping to avoid the cycle of euphoria and loneliness.

Priest says, "The answer to your first question is easy. All souls are counted. God made you as certainly as he made me."

Clint is elated at Priest's conclusion but needs more details. "What do you mean?"

"Clint, you have told me that you have done much reading in your quest to understand yourself. Have you ever read Jung?"

"Of course," Clint replies.

"Well, he used a term called 'throwness' to refer to circumstances one is born into. By that I mean poverty or wealth, ethnicity, war during the 1940s or Italy during the Renaissance."

"Yes, I understand," Clint says.

Priest continues, "The Ancients believed that after death we choose the circumstances of our next incarnation. We choose suffering sometimes if we have caused it or if we need to understand it. We choose again and again to be with souls with whom we are pleased. Sometimes they are our parents, sometimes a coworker. Do you understand?"

Clint is impatient. "Yeah, so?"

"Clint, if we can pick the circumstances of our arrival, becoming an African, a female or an orphan, why not a Clone?"

Clint rises from his chair fiercely, "Are you saying I did this to myself!"

Priest remains seated and calm.

"I am saying that civilizations advance and that this is no surprise to the God of the universe. Many souls are choosing this mode of birth for its greater challenges. Please sit down, and I won't keep you much longer."

Reluctantly, Clint returns to his seat.

"Our soul's purpose is to learn and to spread love. It is through the circumstances of our many existences that we truly understand. Once we do, we cannot be beguiled by demons or appearances. Yes, you chose this existence and I sense that you have arrived at your true destiny. You are blessed; you are where you should be."

"Are you saying that God wanted me to kill those people?" Clint asks.

"No," Priest replies. "I said you chose. God gave us the power to choose, more power than you think."

"And what about my soul?"

"For what you have done, you must pay; for what you will do, you will prosper."

The band is packing up. There are still groups scattered about not wanting to leave. Two waitresses sit at a table counting their tips. Clint has more questions but understands his life in a way he never did before. He is angry but grateful to the tall thin man sitting beside him.

Priest looks at him deeply and asks, "Are you ready to go?"

"Yes," Clint replies. "More than ever."

After a quick and quiet drive, Clint arrives at Sara's hotel room. She opens the door and lets him in. After taking his coat, she caresses his face. "Did you get what you needed?"

"Yes," Clint replies. "Part of me wishes I had met him a long time ago, but I guess I realize that I would not have been ready to hear what he had to say."

Realizing that time is short, Sara says coyly, "Are you ready for what I have to say?"

Clint smiles slightly but there is no eye contact. "You know, earlier all I could think about is us being together; now I am preoccupied with the things I have just learned."

"Come to bed," she says. "When our naked flesh intertwines you will be the same man you always were. How did you say: Like an animal after its meat. You will have me once this way and we will both be beasts. Then I will show you a more spiritual way of lovemaking. There will be stillness and pleasure, ecstasy and understanding. This will fortify what you have learned today and forever unite for you, spiritual and physical pleasure."

Sara is right. They experience the totality of pleasure, from its most savage to its most glorious. In the morning instead of feeling drained his body, mind and spirit have been energized.

For breakfast, she makes drinks of carrot juice, apple and honey. "It will be all right, Clint," she says reassuringly.

"Yes, I know it will be, Sara. I have just lived the most incredible 24 hours of my life. My existence has been anything but dull and uneventful, but with you, Priest, and my brother, it's amazing. I have cleared away the ghosts of my past, fallen in love for the first time and truly found God, all in one marvelous day."

Chapter Thirteen

It is a sunny day with forceful winds and occasional darkness. The outdoor stage where the President will speak is sturdy and adorned with bright colors, six chairs and a microphone. Tall speakers are tilted out toward a lawn where bleachers are placed. On the outskirts of the field are dense rows of trees. The songs of orange, red and black birds are heard in the distance as is the sound of wind gusting through the trees.

It is Fall, and the occasional sound of dead leaves scraping across the concrete walkway intrudes upon the serenity of morning. At this site thousands have jubilantly tossed their graduation caps, embarking on uncertain futures.

The crowd that will attend today has not yet left their homes. Light has barely ascended and Daniel Bloom and his men are combing the area for signs of danger. They look for explosive devices planted in the ground or signs of recent digging. They insure that no helicopter or small plane flights have been scheduled in this air space. They have investigated all the students in the dormitories nearest the area and have placed Kevlar in the decorative awning above the stage. They will have agents in the crowd who are undercover, including three children specially trained in crowd cover. Daniel will anticipate and improvise. He will weave an invisible cocoon that the public will never see.

In Maryland, the Replica Resistance is ready. This event has been planned for months. Leaders from all across the country have been organizing in secret. They met Clones in bars, on buses and in eateries. They quietly built their numbers and their wealth with the help of some human supporters. They have a prepared list of demands:

No longer being used for spare parts
No more rapes or beatings
Independence from human masters
The ability to charge a human with a crime
Human wages

They have printed quotes from the Bill of Rights and the Constitution on their signs and they are energized. They have lived their pain in isolation for too long. Here surrounded by the faithful, they can express their views without fear. Here, their voices shout songs of freedom. Here in this enclave by the sea, they dare to dream of justice.

Paul shares some final thoughts. "My brothers and sisters, we have a huge responsibility today. We must risk our freedom for the freedom of others. We must fight for those who dare not make eye contact when spoken to, for those who work 15-18 hour days for one tenth of the minimum wage and for those men and women who are disposable pleasures for the sick and twisted fantasies of cruel masters. We fight for those who lie in the pits with their organs removed. We fight for our rights, for dignity and for self-determination."

They applaud.

"We also fight for a country that has lost its way. We fight for America. As the nation's most downtrodden, poverty stricken and oppressed we must be America's moral compass. Clones must show America how to regain its compassion. We must challenge her once again to live her grand ideals, to pursue her nobler causes.

"It will be difficult since times are so hard for everyone, but it is during these times that true character is revealed. We will not live in a nation that is petty, selfish, fearful and cruel; it our duty to show everyone a better way.

"We will be strong and defiant in our struggle; we will not relent. We will also be wise. We will be noble and we will be generous. Others will respect our dignity and discipline as we face an overwhelming and sometimes amoral opposition.

"We are few; they are many; and they control the public voices. But today's event is one the world will watch 'live'. The perception people have of us today may determine the course of our struggle. People must both pity and admire us. It is a delicate matter. I know you can do it.

"Remember, we must hate the sin and not the sinner. We will show those in power that what we ask is reasonable in a Christian nation. We will allow them to see the shame of what they have done and allow them to act as if they are generous for removing their barbarism. Ours will be the push that swings the pendulum back to justice and all will benefit.

"We will embrace the causes of Blacks, Latinos, Gays and the poor Whites who rejected our cause. We will show them that all movements for freedom from oppression deserve compassion. We will show them that morality and enlightenment transcend simply fighting for your own group. We will remain the independent thinkers. We will stop Americans from being a nation of clones."

After Paul speaks, there is thunderous applause. One of the organizers tells the audience:

"You will be given specific instructions at the event, since there are always spies in any organization worth having. Let me simply say that I assure you our voices will be heard!"

Paul and the others begin assembling the faithful.

In D.C., Walt has just finished a Secret Service briefing with Bloom's friends JD and Mike. They invite Walt to join them in Mike's office and he agrees. The office is less lavish than Walt expects although not spartan by any means. They sit down and Mike asks for their food orders and gives them to his secretary. "They make a good breakfast over there. You should like it, JD." "Walt, I can't comment on the grapefruit and croissant, I don't ever think I've had that," JD chimes in. "That must be that brunch food, it is kinda late."

"Ha ha," Walt says. "Just trying to keep my belly off the floor."

Mike says, "You look like you're in pretty good shape. But how much can ya bench press off grapefruit?"

"200 pounds, even at this age," Walt says proudly.

Mike says, "JD is skin and bones and he can lift that."

"Hell, my Ma can lift 225," JD quips. They laugh. JD continues, "My Grandpa lived to 93 offa hooch, biscuits and molasses. Why should I mess with success?"

"I thought your Grandfather owned a farm," Walt says. "He must have grown up on fresh vegetables and grains and maybe fresh eggs and free range chicken. You can have a drink and a biscuit if you're eating like that."

JD smiles. "Yeah, but the way I said it sounds like more fun, don't it?"

Mike's competitive urges are emerging. "I still say that is a pitiful amount to bench press. Let's hit the gym after we eat."

Walt replies, "With all the crap you guys are eating, you won't be able to move out of your seat."

Mike says, "No, that's a Black thing. A good Irishman could be in a pie eating contest and a football game the same day."

Walt thinks, *Why do these guys always have to go to race? By next week he will be figuring how to use nigger in a sentence and expect me not to be insulted 'cause he is my friend and not a racist.* Walt says, "Woo, that's impressive." He then looks at Mike's beer belly. "How many pies have you eaten today?"

JD notices the change in tone. "Alright, ladies, you can compare peckers some other time. Lets take care of business."

Mike smirks and reluctantly lets it go. He knows he could take this guy down, with or without a badge. That's all he was saying. Why should he have to walk on eggshells? He thinks, *You mean I can't say Black without reviving slavery? It's not like I said nigger.* Mike looks at Walt and says, "Maybe next time."

JD is thinking that he had made peace with this kind of crap a long time ago. There is some White trash and some Black trash, and most come from families where they never had a chance. It's not about color; it's about opportunity, education and parenting.

We should have changed things in the housing projects and in the trailer parks. No, instead we were helping the rich and the defense industry. Like children, we were so scared that others were getting something that we didn't have that we allowed programs that helped the poor and middle-class to disappear.

We were not looking when poverty became greater in the suburbs than in the cities. We allowed our hates and fears and distrust of people different than us to destroy our wealth and our character.

JD asks, "Where's the food, Mike? I thought you had some pull in these parts."

The food arrives moments later.

Walt asks Mike, "Can we go over the plan again?"

Mike gets serious. "Walt, you're ready; you'll do fine out there."

Clint knows he is being watched. He eluded the agents who were following him two days ago and then buried his cell phone along the side of the road. He had taken this precaution when he went to find Sara at what turned out to be Paul's house. He knew they would use the cell's signal to find him and he did not want to be found.

Later, he knew they would be watching Sara and would have seen him when he arrived at her hotel. He didn't mind that. He also didn't mind if they identified Priest. They would assume that he wanted some spiritual guidance before this virtual suicide mission. He thought everyone would be safe.

He is quite sure that he has not been seen with Paul.

Now comes the hard part. Under close scrutiny, he must appear to be preparing to kill the President while actually saving him. It is now 11:00. The President is due to arrive at 3 o'clock.

His plan is simple. Two weeks earlier he had compromised the computer system for Hamilton Allied Heating & Air, a regional provider for air conditioning and heating services. They thought that making their drivers' destinations, response time and schedules available to drivers and to headquarters would improve efficiency, so they created online access. Efficiency improved but it also let Clint know where he could find their trucks at any given time. He would arrive there today as a repairman to fix a problem with the heat in the building.

He had also visited the dormitory two weeks earlier, feigning interest in a girl named Victavia. She was socially withdrawn and barely attractive, a willing victim for Clint's aggressive charm. She invited him into the dormitory and they laughed and looked intensely into each others eyes until he could see the effect of the sedative he had given her rock her eyeballs to the back of her head.

Once she was out cold, he cautiously made his way into the hallway. He inserted a device into the heating system that made the heat in the building unbearable, and timed it to take effect at 2:00 on the day of the President's visit. He would appear at the dormitory, seemingly on legitimate business, at 2:45. He would undergo a through scan of his van and of his person to enter the grounds. After the scan, he would head straight for the dormitory and proceed to Victavia's room. After she greeted him he would knock her unconscious. He'd remove the missile launcher he placed in her hollowed-out bedpost and bring it out to the truck surrounded by what looked like a rusty pipe.

With his weapon secured, he planned drive to the closet point possible, without arousing suspicion, and fire the missile near the stage.

He is sure that there are secondary assassins who will insure the President's death if he fails. Defense is prepared to explain that the lone gunman broke into an armory weeks ago and stole a missile launcher. One has already been reported missing from Ft. Hood. He is also sure that he is being watched, so he must appear to do everything that is planned while neutralizing the secondary assassin and saving the President. This will therefore be one of his most challenging missions. He is pleased that he is prepared to die.

Chapter Fourteen

"You rape, you kill and maim, stop America's worldwide shame." "Stop the tra-ge-dy in the land of the free." Clones are chanting and marching behind police barricades. They shout at the top of their lungs, frustrated that they are positioned so far away from the stage. They are also the victims of a smaller counter-demonstration. The counter-protesters call them every vile name imaginable as they shake their fists and raise signs that read: "I'm unique, you're a freak" and "Mankind=brave hearts, Clones=spare parts."

To make matters worse it seems that about a dozen of their number are missing and Paul is nowhere to be found.

Near the stage, extra bleachers have been added to accommodate the larger than expected crowd. Additional spectators are being allowed to sit on the grass but not allowed to bring their own chairs. There are several undercover Secret Service people, including J.D. and Mike. J.D. has a rambunctious young boy with him who runs everywhere, and JD doesn't seem to be able to control him. The boy is subjected to polite smiles or angry glares from the people he runs into or speaks to.

On stage, Walt is already seated with the other four dignitaries. He looks at the empty chair, the one the President will occupy in a few moments as he waits to be introduced. He looks around and sees Sewell in the VIP section and waves. Senator Townsend is also present and in the company of one of the most beautiful women he has ever seen.

The sky is clear but thunder is booming, as out of place on this clear day as Walt feels on this stage. He is using all his training and focus, wanting to do a good job and hoping nothing will go wrong. The college president is speaking at the podium. He is saying what an honor it is for the President to be here, blah, blah, blah . . . .

Mike has been here before. The job is adrenalin, observation, instinct, focus and experience. No one else has his passion and tenacity. Bloom sees the big picture; he is the strategist, while Mike handles the details. His gut tells him when something is out of place. Although everything looks perfect today, he doubles his communication with staff. He knows better than to bother Daniel until he has something specific, something more than a hunch.

Daniel Bloom sees the terrain and logistics of a job the way Mozart sees music. It is a gift that he is grateful for but has never quite understood. He has just received the message that the President is ten minutes away. He will arrive on time. Daniel dislikes on-time arrivals because the President arriving early or late can foul up the plan of potential assassins. Unfortunately, this appearance is being televised live, so it must start on time. He relays the President's arrival time and his people make their preparations.

Clint has already returned to the truck with the missile launcher. He closes the locks on the doors and goes to the back of the truck. He removes the metal casing surrounding the missile launcher. He places it close to the back of the passenger seat and closes the van's inner door. He starts the van and lets it idle. It is 12 minutes to three. He listens on the radio for the President's arrival. He waits until he hears the college president end his speech with, "Ladies and gentlemen, it is my pleasure to introduce the President of the United States."

"Thank you all for coming here today," the President begins. "Let's keep our fingers crossed and our umbrellas ready; the weather seems as uncertain as the last congress. I also want to thank everyone who is listening in homes across the world. I invite everyone to join me and the new Congress in creating sweeping economic and policy changes that will reverse the course of the last 20 years.

"How have we come to this? We were the most prosperous nation in the world. From north and south, east and west, immigrants came here to find opportunity and prosperity. We went from being the world's largest benefactor to being the nation with the most debt.

We have not always treated our immigrants well. We made mistakes of ignorance domestically and abroad, but no nation has ever worked harder to correct and remedy our failures.

"Today we deny our citizens the very rights we promote abroad. We force-fed the world democracy while our citizens went hungry, starving for the rights our forefathers shed blood for. We have more people in our jails than anywhere in the world. We have killed more people in war in the last twenty years than any other western nation, yet we have more millionaires and billionaires than anywhere else. We have lost our way.

"Our Neo-Churches promote war when we need love. They are against government programs that help the poor and our vanquished middle class. They ignore the health crisis that has led to rampant disease in our cities and rural areas. The suburbs, once bountiful evidence of the American dream, are now facades eaten away by debt. Neo-Churches don't see the unaborted babies crying and they appear deaf to Christ's teaching.

"Our beneficent rich do much, but there is too much to do. So government must again protect its citizens from the excesses of organized greed. We must again reign in corporate America and an unaccountable and expansionist defense industry."

As the President speaks, twenty-one Clones, scattered in the bleachers, unfurl the signs hidden inside their shirts, stand up and shout, "Free Clones now!" As they chant, they move down from the bleachers and those who are on the lawn join them. As they move forward Mike tells his men to move in as he races toward them. JD grabs the two Clones closest to him and by the force of his voice and bearing moves them away from the crowd and makes them sit in place. Mike comes in swinging and subdues two more. The other agents in the crowd takes out five.

The police Commander asks Daniel what he should do. The Secret Service men on stage are about to grab the President and take him away, but he waves them off, insistently.

Just as the President begins to reassure the crowd, a missile explodes behind the bleachers. The crowd screams and surges ahead. People run every which way, trampling each other in their panicky efforts to avoid the danger. Several people notice a van speed through the trees to the edge of the crowd. No one sees a man quickly discard his coveralls and run with the crowd.

The Clones who were demonstrating join the Clones who were in the bleachers. They are behind the police who have left them to run toward the stage and assist the Secret Service. The counter-demonstrators see this and attack all the Clones they can, even though they are outnumbered.

Walt keeps his eye on the President. Two Secret Service men have the President in hand. He is no longer resisting. Walt hears thunder again, then sees one of the Secret Service men drop. Walt remembers what he was taught. He crouches down and looks momentarily at the fallen Secret Service man. He has been shot in the forehead, apparently from the front. It is a small hole, indicating that it came from short range.

He rolls toward the President in case another shot is coming. It does and hits the second agent who was standing in front of the President. Walt jumps up and pushes the President down. He faces front with his gun drawn, never seeing the third shot or the vacant look in Sewell's eyes as he pulls the trigger oblivious to the chaos surrounding him.

Clint shoots Sewell in back of the head; his vacant eyes now stare up from the freshly cut grass. Clint feels two bullets hit his vest. The assassin assigned to kill him is dressed as a cop. He would have finished Clint except Clint has his gun already drawn and manages to shoot him in the leg and then the face. More Secret Service men race to the stage. Clint runs around the side of the stage out of view of cameras and law enforcement. His shooting of Norman Sewell and the cop-assassin have been recorded live and now Clint or Paul will be identified as a cop killer.

When the bullets hit Clint, Paul grabs his chest. He knows that Clint's life is in danger. He and the other Replicas follow Paul who sees an empty van with the keys inside. He and as many of the others as can fit crowd into the van.

Clint is running from four policemen who are clearly out of breath and two Secret Servicemen. He had hoped to enter the crowd that is now headed in the opposite direction toward the parking lot where their vehicles are. Paul speeds past the weary police officers and picks up Clint in the van. Paul evades the Secret Servicemen. Clint shouts "Stop!" which startles Paul. Clint then embraces him and Paul can feel his shirt become wet. He looks down and sees Clint's blood drip on his chest.

Clint releases him and says, "I must save Sara; they will kill her!"

Paul tries to reassure him. "Clint, she was with Senator Townsend; the Secret Service probably picked them up right after the President."

That makes sense, Clint thought. *She will be safe. This isn't personal. She's a Senator's daughter; they must know that by now. It makes no sense to kill her, especially if I am dead, and it feels like I am dying.*

Paul says, "We need to get you to a hospital."

"What hospital can you take a man to with a bullet in him after an event like this?" Clint asks.

Paul thinks for a moment. "I will call Priest; he will know what to do."

Clint says, "Good, but make the call with one of their phones."

Someone in the back of the van hands Paul a cell-phone.

Somehow they made it safely to a Healer who is also a doctor. He is a friend of Priest, who has not yet arrived. The Replicas from the van and several others are there and are involved in their own discussions of the day's events. Some huddle around the radio.

"Today terrorists attempted to kill the President of our country. This brazen attack was conducted with the apparent cooperation of radical Clones who helped the assassin escape.

"If the President is not safe, no one can safe. We must be willing to sacrifice in order to be safe. Members in Congress have proposed making the draft age 16 and the four great corporations have contracted with our government to guarantee our protection for one year for the reasonable cost of $50 billion. This is wonderful news because, as we know, business can do it better than government. Our hearts are glad that no harm has come to the President and we hope that this tragic experience in which dozens were killed by the terrorist bomb will make him reconsider his so-called people policies in favor of increased security."

Priest has now arrived with Sara. Clint sits up as the Healer attempts to restrain him. "Sara, you shouldn't be here," He says.

He sees Senator Townsend arrive as well and feels better about her safety. She looks at his wound and is deeply concerned because he has lost a lot of blood.

A few of the Replicas come over to console Paul. "It must be difficult to lose a twin brother."

Paul says, "He is not a twin. I am his Clone."

They look astonished but say very little. They return to their group and sounds of disbelief are heard.

Daniel Bloom can not believe the reports he is hearing on the news but knows he can not tell the media the truth.. He is thrilled that the President is alive and pleased with himself that he thought of having Walt up on the stage. He is also glad that Walt has survived. Daniel wishes he had kept the listening devices on Norman though. He would have been able have avoided much of this. Walt tells Daniel how stunned he is at Norman being the shooter and how sad he is for Norman's family. This will certainly kill his mother.

Walt says to Daniel, "It doesn't surprise me though. If you can betray your people, you can betray your country."

Bloom doesn't tell Walt that they used some chemicals and brainwash techniques on Sewell since Walt's basic point is true. If he had not been weak and gullible he would not have been so easily turned.

The missile has been traced back to Victavia's room but it did not alt hit anyone. The police have killed several demonstrators including counter-demonstrators who were being lauded as "Heros on the front lines for freedom" on the AM stations. JD is on his way back to Mississippi and Mike and many others are still searching for Clint.

Clint calls Priest, Paul and Sara to him as he feels his life slipping away. As he attempts to utter his last words, several Replica Resistance members approach to tell Paul that they do not want a Clone of a Clone as the head of their organization.

His second in command speaks, "It's not that we don't think you're as good as we are; we just don't think we can expand this movement to include Replicas of Replicas."

Paul waves them away as he struggles to hear Clint's voice. With blood gurgling in his throat and surrounded by those he loves he says, "I see a tunnel, Priest. Where is the light?"

His eyes fix on Sara and with a look of yearning, Clint falls silent. Minutes later the police enter the building.

... END

Printed in the United States
114057LV00004B/1-198/P